To: Kare
from: Chris

Theo Brand's
6ᵗʰ Symphony

Christopher O'Hanlon

To Melanie with love

CONTENTS

TRIESTE

1

How did I find myself in that predicament?

Alone. In Trieste. A stranger. Hundreds of miles from home. Trying to keep up with the girl who was gaining on me because she had been in this kind of wind before. I dreamt of it afterwards. In the dream the *Bora* wind was the god Aeolus from my school primer, unseen but heard, omnipresent and omnipotent (and any other 'omni' words you care to throw in), beside himself with fury, throttling the trees until the boughs shook, branches lopped off or snapping, whole trees upended. She (the girl I mean) knew the ropes, quite literally – that you had to hang on for dear life to the *Bora* ropes and inch your way forward. My hat had deserted me in the first gust, before I had even crossed the station forecourt, taking flight the coward, perhaps frightened off by what lay in store for me. What a predicament!

I clung to the promises made at the station, "Pension, very good price, very close by, sprechen Sie Deutsch?'

Why? When Gerda had reserved me a room in a perfectly decent hotel, to where my trunk had already been directed. What a mistake it had been. How I regretted now giving Hinteregger the slip just because he had been a little too attentive, too solicitous and had witnessed my humiliation in front of the border guard. He had come to the rescue when the man had to ask for a second time, 'Purpose of visit?' and I was unable to give a proper account of myself Hinteregger would have found me a cab to the right hotel.

Each time we came to a crossing, we were buffeted and blown off course. The wind came at me like... like an *Acousticon,* the hearing contraption that, when I switched it on for the first time had frightened the life out of me with its whooshing and roaring.

Loose stones scuttled across the street, tiles fell, shop signs and street lamps swayed. We too were staggering like drunks on a spree.

Patrizia was the name of the girl. I had asked her when she looked me boldly in the eye and gave my arm a squeeze – a rush to familiarity that thrilled me. 'Come, come Signore.' They had my suitcase and were taking it somewhere. That was all I knew – and that they were gaining on me. How often have I said to my inner voice, "Never again. Let me wriggle out of it one more time."

Albrecht had warned me, that last night in the kneipe, licking weissbier from his tangled moustache, 'If you really are set on going ahead with it, don't let your guard down for a second – remember you're in Italy, no matter what the Austrians might think.'

'Very close by,' she had lied.

No ropes as we began the slow climb, no streets either but unnamed dead ends and blind alleys. I recall peeling walls, forgotten posters flapping at the edges. Definitely not an area of hotels and pensions. They stopped, the girl and her companion, under an archway – a tunnel reeking of piss – and appeared to confer. Were they waiting for the confederates who I suspected were lurking in the shadows?

My notions of Italians up to that point were sketchy and anecdotal, derived mostly from the bloodcurdling histories of the Renaissance I had devoured at school: sacrilege on top of murder, hot-blooded assassins, specialists of the vendetta lying in wait for their victims in dark alleys, poisoned goblets, concealed stilettos. Was this how Kolya had met his end? Would they rob me too, knock me unconscious, slice me open? I clung to my burlap.

2

An orange light falling across the street signalled an open door.

'I'm sorry to say Frau Wirtin, but there's been a misunderstanding. I hoped for a *pensione*, not an *osteria*.' I remembered to remove my hat, spoke as clearly and distinctly as I was able and smiled reassuringly to put her at her ease. Monsieur Tobler at the *Ecole Muets-Sourds* would have been proud of me.

The landlady brushed my objection aside with a shrug: '*Pensione, osteria,* what's in a name?'

In fact it was neither, and me getting on my high horse wouldn't have made a groschen's difference. But what now seems blindingly obvious, at the time completely passed me by. What I took to be an *osteria* that laundered clothes as a matter of course was actually a laundry pure and simple. The spare room was assigned to paying guests to help this poor family get by. This explained Patrizia roaming as far as the railway station in search of a customer, the baby suckling at her mother's breast in broad daylight, grannie blundering into my room when I had only a hand towel to cover my privates, the little boy who joined me for breakfast. The *Gatto Negro* was the name, not of these premises but of the adjoining tavern which kept me awake for most of the night.

'Colazione, pranzo, cena – alles hier, richtig, jederzeit?

She was offering me the key – here, in the palm of my hand, signore, take it. So I did.

Then it was cash up front. I got into a right old muddle counting out the amount, the bill being made out in florins while my bank notes were crisp, brand new kroners. It didn't help that I only knew the rate of exchange for kroners and German marks. The consequences were as foreseeable as they were disastrous and for days afterwards I winced at the thought of it.

All the time we were being observed by a little girl of four or five clinging to the folds of her mother's skirts while she gazed up at me with cow-like brown eyes, her grubby thumb planted resolutely in her mouth. I was reminded of her when I saw the tawdry oil paintings for sale at the foot of the Spanish Steps in Rome, mawkish portraits with titles like "Little girl lost" and "Have you seen my mama?"

That first night in Trieste was uncomfortable to say the least. Even so, had it not been for the insistence of Herr Hinteregger, I doubt whether I would have taken the trouble to write an official letter of complaint about standards in The Black Cat. I dashed this off while enjoying a beer on the Piazza della Borsa (Restaurant Dreher, opposite the Exchange). I can be certain of this because I made notes on a sheet of headed notepaper:

Under heading 'General'

Peeling wallpaper owing to damp

Window sash – defective, therefore room stuffy

Washbasin – too small for the purpose

One grey blanket (stolen from the local hospital? - the sewn label had been ineffectively removed)

Banister in advanced state of decay. Wobbles, positively dangerous. Wood rot?

Towels – Hand towel grimy and threadbare

Soap (carbolic – human hair embedded within).

Toilet paper – available only on request!

Water supply (confined to common bathroom) – flow uneven, rust deposits.

At Hinteregger's suggestion I sent copies of the finished letter to the *Bürgermeister,* the Chief of Police and the German Consul, together with a note on Travellers' Advice to the Baedeker offices in Leipzig (this on my own initiative). Kolya's brother-in-law, Hoffmann, scoffed at Hinteregger's advice. In his view, the correct way to pursue a complaint was to go immediately to the nearest police station and make a written statement; better still, to report the matter to a constable and insist on taking him directly to the "scene of the crime". As it was (and as Hoffmann had predicted) all I got were platitudes and expressions of sympathy. The first of the replies (from the Consul) and far and away the most sympathetic, was forwarded to me in Tivoli; the mayor's office provided advice on tipping, along with some slyly unflattering observations on the Italian character; while the police had, despite "the most exhaustive researches" been unable to find any trace of the osteria mentioned by the complainant.

3.

I suppose even I would find it difficult to track The Black Cat to its lair today. All I can remember with certainty is a peculiar Roman arch, abutting a wall that looked as if it had once belonged to an ancient aqueduct or theatre. This arch appeared on countless postcards and, according to the author of *Trieste and its Environs* (Vienna, 1905), had some vague association with King Richard the Lion Heart, hence the name *Arco di Riccardo*. I have a particularly nightmarish memory of wild cats in the vicinity, picking their way through rubble after being chased by waiters from the outdoor table of a nearby tavern, where they made a great nuisance of themselves scavenging shrimps or clams.

There was a world of difference between the old part of town where according to the guidebook, "The Austrians have made no impression whatsoever" and the new *Theresienstadt*, which includes the waterfront as far as the port. "Here, by contrast the streets are broad and splendid and laid out with geometrical logic and the overriding smells are of pretzels and freshly-ground coffee. With the notable exceptions of the Schlossburg and the Cathedral it also has most of the sights."

At the barber's in the Tergesteo (the shopping arcade which takes its name from the Latin for the city) I waited my turn. The morning edition was in front of me. I picked it up: "Balkan Crisis

Latest". I read as far as the "Sanjak of Novipazar", then gave up. Why do foreign correspondents always feel the need to impress you with their local knowledge by throwing in obscure terminology or place names? First it was Bosnia-Herzegovina, then Scutari, now this Sanjak of Novipazar. Not that I read the serious papers much, as a rule, the foreign pages hardly at all.

In Trieste I took more of an interest because some of these Balkan lands were virtually on the doorstep. Dalmatia, for instance, where the people were mainly Croats – the packet steamer would take you all the way along the coast to Durazzo, but no further as the postal service had been suspended.

Later, I asked my sister Gerda to look up the Sanjak of Novipazar in Brockhaus. She wrote back that there was a music hall song about it going the rounds, set to nonsensical rhyming couplets. How did it go? "It sounds like a drink at the bar" was part of it. "No wonder the Austrians are hiking far from the Sanjak of Novipazar" Boom Boom.

Who remembers it now - or Scutari and those other places, for that matter? Sarajevo, that was the place they ought to have been keeping their eyes on; Sarajevo and those bloody Serbs.

The customer sitting alongside me gave me a nudge – 'your turn'. I took my place in the swivel chair, easing my way into the seat, I asked for a haircut but was given a shave. The barber was an

Italian although the shop went by the name of Schroeder and had an Imperial "by appointment" sign in the window. He spoke German after a fashion, his pronunciation guttural in all the wrong places, his vowels stretching like elastic bands. He tied the apron too tightly so that the ribbon chafed my neck and constricted my throat. Only after the chair tilted back into the upright position was I able to pick up bits and pieces of the conversation going on around me. The fellow in the other chair had his paper opened at the financial page, which was predicting a further rush on stocks in Skoda and Krupp, while other share prices were tumbling. That explained the gloomy faces outside the Trieste Stock Exchange.

I scanned the mirror for further clues, quickly realising that more would be gained from studying the barber's gestures than from reading his lips. Which led me to wonder whether using sign language here would attract less attention than at home. My companion in the neighbouring chair drew our attention to a passer by who I assumed was a friend or business acquaintance but, it turned out, they were discussing the fellow's headgear. Unfortunately, the pitch or the timbre maybe, of the electric clippers was setting my teeth on edge and playing havoc with my residual hearing, so that I missed the first exchanges completely. Then I realised that the point at issue was the colour: whether a fez had to be scarlet. The barber hummed and hahhed but knew no more about fezzes than I did.

Fezzes. I would forget all about them and then one day, there they were again – in black and white on cinema screen. Men in fezzes on the steps of Sarajevo town hall as the Archduke left for his ill-fated drive, among the well-wishers in the crowd and, later, laying hands on the assassin as he was dragged away to face justice. Trieste appeared too on a newsreel when the funeral cortege passed through on its way back to Vienna. A few flickering images, recognisable in an instant – the Corso, its balconies and window ledges draped in black! I was so excited I shouted out loud, startling my neighbour by grabbing at his arm.

4

My hotel, the Halberleitner (also known as the Central), was only a few minutes' walk from the sea. The building was supposed to remind you of a Venetian palazzo (every building in Trieste was a copy of something) but inside, all was *gemütlich*, starting with the sitting room with its discreetly placed reception desk (fresh flowers every day), chintz-covered armchairs, oriental carpets... An unexpected plus was the freshly roasted coffee, available throughout the day, courtesy of one of the new chromium brewing machines.

To begin with all was confusion thanks to my "no show" the night before. The advance reservation made for me by Gerda had been cancelled, my room reallocated. That would have been that had it not been for my trunk awaiting collection in the storeroom. The manager had thought it best to telegraph Berlin for news of me. Now Gerda had got to hear of my inexplicable non-arrival, so that the tone of her telegram, handed over to me once I had finally managed to straighten matters out at the front desk, was frantic. I hastily dropped a postcard in at the express counter to set her mind at rest.

It was while staying at the Halberleitner that I fell in with Lindstrom. I suppose you might have called us chums by the end. Carl (with a "C", he was Swedish) left me his card. He had a job any man might envy – he was a commercial traveller in underclothes "for ladies of fashion and refinement." How he got into this specialised line of work I have no idea but, according to Lindstrom, the demand for such items was insatiable in Russia, the principal market. What gave his firm the edge was that his customers paid no duty, the merchandise being smuggled in, direct from the fashion houses of Paris.

'Most of my clients would kill for a pair of silk stockings.'

Ditto negligees and cami-knickers. Surprisingly these "clients" were not only ladies of leisure with money to burn, but women without titles, or fortunes – the "would-be if-onlys".

'They have the same right to go about in society as the next woman, wouldn't you say?' was Lindstrom's viewpoint and who was I to argue?

It was strictly word of mouth. He would make "home visits" or call at hotels by appointment, pretending if need be that he was a relative or friend of the family. What brought him to Trieste I never thought to ask.

The best time to catch Lindstrom was at breakfast – he never missed, it didn't matter how many beers he'd put away the night before or what time he'd finally crawled into bed. Failing breakfast (and I often failed) I had to wait until early evening when he could be found at the *Good Shepherd* – a pension just around the corner, popular with "knights of the road". (Lindstrom was particularly drawn to it because they had Krumbacher on tap.)

We became fast friends in a short time but I didn't take to his fellow reps and would go to considerable lengths to steer him away from the other favourite watering hole with commercial travellers, Dreher's on Piazza della Borsa. It was a simple matter of turning right rather than left out of the Via San Niccolò and heading in the direction of the Serbian Church. A sly trick I used was to persuade him that the doe-eyed flower-seller there had taken a fancy to him. The poor girl – what she made of this ruse of mine I can't imagine.

We were heading for 'Baby Dreher's' which was busy only at lunch time when the news hounds from the offices of *Il Piccolo* were driven to take refuge there by the Austrian police who carried out regular raids on the building in the hope of finding inflammatory (i.e. anti-Austrian) material. By the evening we had the "snug" more or less to ourselves. I can still see the brewery crest – a delirious cherub, bareback riding a mythical beast with a passing resemblance to a goat.

'Then, once you get your foot in the door you show them the French goods, you know – the really naughty stuff.'

Lindstrom had a fiancée hidden away somewhere, Riga I think — a bit of alright by the sound of it, enough of the goods at any rate to find work as a calendar girl.

'Let's see her then,' I asked one evening, curious to discover whether the goods matched the sales pitch. I was expecting him to pull out his wallet; instead he delved deep into a pocket for an empty tin of boot polish. 'That her,' he said, pointing to the lid with his forefinger. I held it up to the light — chestnut hair, bright blue eyes, rosy cheeks, winsome smile, it wasn't much to go on.

'Don't you have anything else, a picture or something?'

'Not on me,' he said, a bit deflated. 'It's her colouring men rave about.'

He was making a case because he valued my opinion. He had got it into his head that I was a regular Lothario.

I'll say one thing for her, she was a good sport, this girl of his. When she was a bit tipsy, she was quite happy to model the undies for him — 'give them a bit of an airing' as he put it, with a sly wink. He had other plans for her; like hiring a private room in a hotel and allowing invited guests to pay for the privilege of seeing her strut about demonstrating his range of sex toys (the 'naughty stuff'): battery-powered 'manipulators', erotic watches, a pair of wax figures copulating in a musical box — I saw all these and more besides.

'You don't think people will take her for a tart?' I suggested, pretending to think for a moment as I sipped my beer.

'Not necessarily. Because she's got class, Eva has.'

Eva sounded to me like a stage name.

'It might be crossing a line,' I added, trying to be helpful.

'Crossing a line?'

'The tightrope of respectability.' A happy phrase that came from nowhere.

'Ah, now I get you. You mean, calendars are one thing...'

I smiled and nodded in what I hoped was a worldly-wise, way before ordering another round of drinks.

5

Carl's last night was a bit of a blank. The following day, when I emptied out my pockets, I found loose change (but where had the Swiss francs come from?) an unopened box of Fromm's rubbers and, stuffed into the pocket of my overcoat, a pair of *Directoire* knickers which came out crumpled and twisted, as if I had used them to strangle someone. What was missing was the photograph which had brought me to Trieste in the first place. I panicked as I tried desperately to piece together the events of the previous evening. How had I got home after leaving the others in *The Golden Key* or was it the other knocking shop on the Via della Pescheria?

I had a vague recollection of showing the picture to Lindstrom in Dreher's, passing off Kolya's girl as my own squeeze. The idiot was too far-gone to notice Konradi's proprietary arm on her chair back. The next thing I remembered was standing in a pool of light, possibly the doorway of the American cinema, and watching a set-to between a gang of rough houses, well soused and in a very truculent mood and ratings in the Austrian navy. In the middle of the ruckus a pair of plods appeared on the scene, truncheons at the ready. I was not alone in the cinema doorway but for some reason (maybe he blew a whistle and I failed to respond), one of the cops singled me out and demanded to see my papers. Now I wondered whether the photograph had fallen to the pavement, if so I could say goodbye to ever getting it back.

6

I lived for those evenings with Lindstrom and the late breakfasts at the Pole Star or one of the cafes on the Piazza Grande: piping hot coffee with a brandy chaser (it was brighter now, but cold still) with either a fig roll or, if I was really famished, a *presnitz*, a pastry in the shape of a snail with a glaze like a coat of varnish – *buonissimo*! I amused myself by trying to guess the ingredients: almonds, pine nuts, plums, apricots, raisins stewed in Marsala, before checking them off against the wrapper. Even now, if I lick my fingers, it's enough to bring the flavour of the things to mind. Figs were still a novelty for me – of course I had seen them, but never thought I would like them until then.

After breakfast I would wander down to the port and watch the ships. I would consult the schedules and timetables and imagine myself travelling to Port Said (where the figs came from), Constantinople, Bombay or Shanghai. Reviving a childhood habit I came to memorize the names of the ships – the *Orient Queen*, the *Thalia* with its stewards' orchestra that serenaded the first class passengers as they boarded, the *Baron Gausch,* the *Prinz Hohenlohe*, even the lowly *Capodistra* which was destined to take me on a day trip to Rovino. I felt the same thrill standing at the quayside here as I had in Hamburg as a small boy. Of a Saturday afternoon, my father, who worked for the Hamburg America Line in the Bureau for the Protection of Emigrants would take me on a tour of the harbour as far as the America Quay, where we would watch the packet steamers preparing to set out for the New World. One time father pointed out a sunburnt peasant girl carrying her ticket in her teeth, and explained that this was to ensure that no one grabbed it from her hand at the last minute. I would stare with amazement at the queues of men and women, Jewish refugees from Russia or Poland lugging the huge cloth bundles that in some cases contained all their worldly possessions. Then, as the tenders and rowing boats took them to the various embarkation points, we would study their faces and try to guess whether they were happy or sad to be leaving. I had a store of sound memories from before my illness that I could call up at a moment's notice and now, in Trieste, I imposed them on my new surroundings: the scrape of shovels, steam hiss, tinny ships' bells, keening gulls, the human hum...

7

One morning I changed my routine to deal with a backlog of correspondence, mainly from Gerda. I bought a packet of postcards with views of the sights and called in at the Post Office for stamps.

I had found just the spot, away from the stiff onshore breezes, and, wrapped up against the cold in overcoat, scarf and gloves was gazing absent-mindedly at the uneven marble flagstones, waiting for the sun to pay its next fleeting visit. The stamps were in pretty colours: blue, orange, lime green, and superimposed was the familiar profile of Emperor Franz Josef, complete with mutton chop whiskers and a laurel crown like Caesar's.

I opened the first letter and found nothing but worrisome queries about invoices, stale news of my dog, Strammer Max (he was missing me) and instructions about buying an alarm clock. I read: 'You left your clock behind and I am wondering how you will manage without it? Any department store, Tietz or Wertheim, will have a good selection. And don't allow yourself to be fobbed off - explain that the bell must be as loud as possible or it will not wake you. Do it today, Theo....'

There were pigeons poking about in the rubbish at the base of the dilapidated fountain a few metres in front of me. One strutted towards me, to investigate my bootlaces perhaps, when the sun came out and the bird's neck shimmered and its iridescence was precious and all mine!

'Please indicate how long you propose staying in Trieste and when you intend travelling on to Tivoli?' Hoffmann's letter jolted me like a final reminder on an outstanding debt. Travelling on? I was barely started.

8

It was late on a Berlin January afternoon when someone had asked for me in the shop – not a customer, a clerk from a firm of solicitors in the city. I left Josef in charge and led the man upstairs. He was explaining how he had tracked me down to the cycle shop on Belle-Alliance Strasse. A codicil to a will had been drawn up in accordance with deathbed instructions. Kolya Konradi was dead? But it was only a few months since our chance meeting on the Lustgarten.

Hearing my old school friend referred to as the deceased came as a bit of a shock.

The gist of what Kolya's brother-in-law had to tell me in the letter the solicitor had brought with him was this: Dying from his injuries in a hospital, sometimes lucid, sometimes in a state of delirium, Kolya had become agitated and mentioned me by name, not once but repeatedly. He meant me to have a box of his mementoes and personal effects and – he was most insistent on this – I would know what to do next.

This was what I was explaining to Gerda as she was peeling carrots for the soup.

Gerda had come round straight after finishing her shift at the hospital and was cooking us both supper, even though I would have been quite happy eating at my local as usual and had not bothered to clean the stove. 'Man does not live by bratwurst and pickled herring alone,' she remarked before setting to work with the scourer. (Adapting biblical tags to everyday situations is a mannerism of hers).

Made of ebony, Kolya's box is heavy to lift, expensive-looking and a bit old fashioned. It was made in Switzerland by Mermod Frères and resembles a clock case, the broken arch and pillar supports reminding me of the entrance to a Greek or Roman temple. The workmanship is first rate, especially the glazing and the fretwork, which is beautifully carved. Opening the lid is difficult as the hinges are a little stiff but inside you find a miniature china doll, dressed in a ballet costume that is all frills and ribbons, probably all the rage forty years ago. You wind the crank at the side and the doll starts to pirouette on its red velvet platform, to a tune Gerda is unable to identify but thinks might be Massenet. To find the objects hidden within, it is necessary to remove two additional lids on either side of the platform.

With the pan on the boil, Gerda and I sat down at the table and emptied out the contents. She spread the items in front of her like a clairvoyant reading the tarot then picked out a heart-shaped locket with a miniature, hand-painted portrait of a young woman. Meanwhile I was sifting through the assorted of medals, foreign coins, a carved bird whistle and other curios. Just then, Gerda pulled on my sleeve and showed me a group photograph taken in a café. I recognised the figure standing behind them as Kolya. There was something else she was trying to tell me: 'It's a case of… *The Mohicans of Paris*, the inspector…'

'Monsieur Jackal?'

'*Cherchez la femme!*'

She was right, Kolya's hand was resting on the shoulder of the same crimped-haired beauty that appeared in the locket.

Gerda turned the photograph over. 'Trieste – then that's where you have to start looking.'

9

Which is why I began making the rounds of the cafes. I had recovered the snapshot – there had been no need for panic, Lindstrom had left it with the desk clerk in the hotel. But having no method or system, I was getting nowhere – I would keep going back to the same place, based on no more than a feeling, a hunch: there was a doorframe or fluted column I thought I recognised. The headwaiters struck me as haughty and hard-bitten, so I gave them a wide berth, making a nuisance of myself to the younger men who might well have been still at school when the photograph was taken. Sometimes I presented my reasons as a matter of urgency, at others as a passing fancy. There was, I now see, something bizarre in my fixation with the *Kaffeehäuser* of Theresienstadt - their gilt mirrors, potted plants and comfy banquettes covered in plush red velvet would not have looked out of place in a Viennese coffee house. Now I wonder if the reason I was reluctant to venture into the cafes of the old town was the outside chance of running into the landlady of the Gatto Negro.

Whatever the case, it was in the Orientale that I had one of those head-smacking moments. I was toying with a silver-lipped sugar dispenser while waiting for my *Sachertorte* and slipping into the trancelike state where thoughts are no longer concrete – a bit like when I was a small child and would snatch at soap bubbles only to see them float away from my outstretched hands.

'Sugar doesn't grow on trees,' Gerda had observed, which made me smile as I poured another heaped spoonful into my coffee. It was what she said next which came to me that morning, about there being a stamp on the back of the photograph, with the name and address of the studio. Why else was I in Trieste? They had to keep records for their accounts. And if I could go one better and track down the photographer...

10

Fanucci's Photographic Store and Studio had moved to new premises on the Piazza Ponterrosso, partly obscured by the masts and canvas sails of the schooners and fishing boats moored alongside the Grand Canal. There was a fruit and vegetable market here and freshly-baked bread – *pane di Altamura,* but I was drawn to the craft stalls specialising in Slovenian wooden toys: miniature wheel-barrows and rocking horses, trains and dolls, cockerels and farm animals. I was reminded of my chance meeting with Kolya and his son, shopping for a birthday present at a craft stall on the Lustgarten. The thought of the boy, now without a father, moved me. Was it his presence that had put Kolya off saying what he wanted to say to me as we were about to part for the last time? On an impulse I took out my purse and counted out the money for the pull-along Dalmatian on wheels that had particularly caught my eye.

A shop boy was sweeping the pavement in front of the store as I arrived. You expect such attention to detail from a firm like Fanucci's with a touch of class about it. I was equally impressed with the window display: I liked the way the cameras, spools of film in red and yellow canisters, portraits, wedding albums and postcards with views of the town, could be taken in at a glance without the various product lines being forced to jostle for position, so that even the casual shopper was tempted to stay long enough for one of the items to catch his eye. I made a few notes for future use.

I was about to go inside when I noticed a separate entrance with a sign directing customers to the *atelier* on the fifth floor. I ignored the bell and climbed the stairs, which were steep and sharp-angled, making it hard to be sure of your footing without holding on to the wooden banister. Even then I slipped on the fruit mush that had stuck to the sole of my shoe and which I had to wipe off with a handkerchief.

Through the pane of frosted glass I could make out a blurry figure moving around inside. I was figuring out what to do next when a lantern-jawed man in his forties sprang out, looked to right and left like a villain in a melodrama, before dragging me inside.

Almost the first thing I noticed was the chairs, half a dozen of them arranged in a semi-circle, two of which were occupied. I too was invited to sit down. One punter was a would-be Puccini with a 'tache and a cigar between his teeth, the other a strange-looking individual who hugged a briefcase to his chest while rocking back and forth in his seat. Exactly what kind of show we were in for I had yet to discover but I could see my own expectations writ large on each of their faces.

Meanwhile Fanucci was manoeuvring the scenery, a painted flat depicting the outlook from the balcony of a sultan's palace – an exotic looking garden and a distant seaport.

Next he dragged a green, moth-eaten chaise longue onto the set, also a trellis and a tall fluted column which teetered precariously until I rushed to give him a hand with setting it to rights. I assumed he had used the stepladder, propped up in the corner, to string up the white cotton bed sheets that covered one entire wall. They had been tautened by rolling the tops and bottoms around heavy wooden poles, which acted as weights.

I turned half around to take a closer look at the model who sat with her back to me, wrapped in a blanket and warming her hands at a portable coal heater. She took no interest in Fanucci's comings and goings, except when he got in the way of the fire and she gave the blanket an extra tug.

Fanucci got my attention by tapping me on the shoulder. He wanted the ten Kroner for the show, which he accepted with the complicit smile of a kindly, if roguish uncle.

Only now did the girl stir herself and dispose idly on the chaise longue as if to the manner born, while to augment the natural light funnelling in from the skylight, Fanucci opened a large white parasol and switched on an arc lamp.

Most of the poses took a leaf from the book of Old Masters and even I recognised the nod to Goya in the hands-behind-the-head routine. But she was only her real self between shots when she would chew her nails or jump up in feigned surprise at a spring protruding from the sofa. These girlish antics only drew attention to the dirty feet and the sure want of hips; yet there was something captivating about the way she sipped her glass of Prosecco through a straw, gazing at me doe-eyed while exposing her pink buds.

11

Fanucci emerged from under the blanket for the last time, switched off the lamp and headed for the door. He was all smiles. I loitered in the studio while he shook the hand of each punter in turn, like a clergyman greeting his parishioners after the service.

I was in luck: 'Of course we keep records, signore,' he assured me, but could he take a look at the photograph. The stamp was itself a clue as the colour of the ink had changed from mauve to red when old Fanucci had retired a good eight or nine years previously.

The picture itself he recalled for two reasons; firstly because the photographers were encouraged to identify their work by including something that would serve as a kind of artist's signature; in this case it was the guitar propped up against the leg of the table. There was better news to come – this particular group portrait had got the photographer into trouble with the police as it had apparently been commissioned by one of the leftist parties. When I asked Fanucci if the photographer was by any chance still working in the city, I was told that this Freitas was Portuguese and a stringer employed by *Il Lavoro Triestino*. One final detail: Fanucci did not recognise Kolya, but he was able to identify the blue stocking wearing the pince nez as a Comrade Ana, a well-respected doctor employed by one of the local hospitals. This didn't seem to fit but I thought it best not to push my luck. He sat me down beside him on the sofa and opened a ledger with a black hardboard cover. He was offering me a chance to buy prints of the session. They came in packs of a dozen. There was no obligation, he assured me, and left me to think about it while he began packing up. Elvira was getting dressed again, but seemed in no particular hurry. A kind of encore, perhaps? I ordered the postcards after being persuaded of Fanucci's discretion: plain brown envelope to be picked up at the studio or sent post restante. One more thing, 'The signore would like the postcards tinted by a local colourist, a true artist, *molto distinto*, to make them seem even more true to life?' No, the signore would not like.

12

So I decided to look for the Portuguese, only he found me first. I remember a flash that made my eyes ache, sparks showering over the carpet like a firework fountain. Then, as the smoke began to clear, a shadowy figure materialised, an apparition in a stage show. In one uplifted hand he held a metal rod with a tray top, while the other gripped what looked like a car horn, with wires to a camera resting on a tripod. I fought the urge to run – it would have been difficult in any event, since I was squeezing the doorknob so hard it might have been glued to the palm of my hand. My heart was thumping, my breathing shallow and I had an unpleasant taste in my mouth as if I had been licking metal polish.

'Close the door and keep your hands where I can see them!'

I obeyed without question – as if it was a Luger he was pointing at me, not a Kodak.

This was no in-and-out job – the open drawer, the rug askew under the tripod, the cigarette left smouldering in the ashtray – he was as invasive as the fly that rubs its feelers over your dinner. I had locked the trunk but the photograph of Kolya and his friends was lying on the night table, propped against my shaving mug. I made a grab for it but Freitas guessed what I was up to and got there first. I had to do something to reclaim my territory, so I settled on the ashtray – stubbing out his cigarette for him as he fell awkwardly back into the chair.

What followed was about as dignified as a schoolyard rumble. I felt the familiar constriction in my throat, my gorge rising. Meaning to lunge at him, I tripped on the rug and, while I think he had been expecting something of the sort, it was enough to upset his balance and topple him onto the floor. He simply collapsed under my weight – panting, wheezing, fighting for air and if he had given me the print there and then, I would have got off him right away instead of keeping up the pressure long enough to jerk back his arm and prize open his fingers. Later I understood the reason for his stubbornness – he believed the print was his by right, the property of an artist!

I had no real idea what was wrong with Freitas physically – it may have been nothing more than undernourishment, the want of a glass of "Cow and Gates wholesome, restorative milk". But from the moment we crashed to the floor together and that fleck of spittle landed on my cheek, I suspected the worst.

A childhood memory was at the root of this anxiety. Mother and I had boarded a tram and I rushed to the front seat to share the driver's-eye view and watch him operate the steering handle. I had barely settled when Mother yanked my arm and dragged me back down the car.

'Didn't you see that man spit into his handkerchief?'

'You can see it in their eyes', she added later for Aunt Nellie's benefit.

A neighbour, not really an auntie, Nellie could only nod solemnly in agreement, 'The hollow look.'

Tuberculosis (or galloping consumption – it always 'galloped' in our house) was "catching", that was the point. Professor Koch had proved it in Berlin – right on our doorstep, you might say.

Not until Freitas had gone did it cross my mind to request they disinfect the room as a matter of urgency. Carbolic is what they use, a special preparation – I read about it in one of the nursing journals Gerda brings home from time to time. Which is all very well but when you think about it, you risk infection every time you step out of the house. Someone sneezes, or stops to ask you for directions, a waitress breathes over your food. It's a lottery. I got rid of the glass Freitas had been drinking from (he had helped himself to a beer in my absence) and, for good measure, threw open the shutters to give the place a decent airing.

13

I could have made a formal complaint. It was more than an intrusion, it was a bloody *break in*. Freitas would have been in the slammer in no time. But then what? I couldn't prove that he had arrived uninvited. After all, it was me who had been making inquiries about him.

'No use making a song and dance about it,' he might have argued: 'I happened to be passing, the door was unlocked so I walked right on in. Anyway, what would have been the point of knocking? I could have been standing there all day. You want to watch yourself, Brand. You'll end up murdered in your bed if you're not careful. You should keep the door locked, even at night.'

My father had a word for this kind of brazenness: *chutzpah*. Handing his coat to my mother as he came in from work, he would exclaim, 'the *chutzpah* of that man!' or 'that Ravenstein certainly has some *chutzpah*'. To which mother would tease him with, 'Where on earth did you pick up Yiddish, the Kovno ghetto?'

Freitas (I was to discover) was a marked man and no stranger to the interrogation rooms and holding cells of Schloss Miramar. They didn't tell you about those in the guidebooks: "A few miles out of town on the coast road, is the palatial former residence of Archduke, later Emperor Maximilian the first, open to the public and well worth viewing. There are splendid vistas from the promontory on to the Adriatic." Nothing about roughing up political prisoners in the cellars.

When I came to understand him better, not to see the world as he saw it, perhaps, but to acknowledge that there was another point of view at least, one deserving of respect for going beyond posturing or bloody mindedness, I found his intransigence liberating.

He was like one of those cursed heroes in Greek mythology, earmarked by the gods for a hard time. Like them I imagine him giving as good as he got, baiting his tormentors with mocking sarcasms, goading them until they gave him the good hiding he craved, his badge of honour. Countless run-ins with the police over the years had cost him his regular job and the best part of his livelihood. The local Socialist newssheet, the only one that would hire him nowadays, paid him a pittance, even while recognising that he was a photographer with talent and a certain flair. He was a good draughtsman too – a gift noted by a priest in Madeira who had set him on the road to what might have been a promising career.

The way Freitas saw it, I was to blame for dropping him in it, just when he was trying to keep a low profile. But how was I to know that there was an informant among the Sandros and Luigis, waiting tables in the cafes where I had been showing Kolya's picture? Even then it didn't seem so much to get worked up about.

The one thing he would never believe was that anyone could be a free agent. So I admitted to being employed by Hoffmann. My blunder with the waiters I offered as evidence of my naivety. What kind of snitch, let alone an agent provocateur would practice his trade so openly, I insinuated slyly. So we struck a deal: money for information. But when I suggested a pub as a place to meet over a beer and a game of billiards, he wanted none of it.

Old Freitas had his own ideas for a rendezvous: the quarry, the aqueduct, the disused Roman cemetery at the back of the Cathedral, the Karst at Villa Opicina – take it or leave it. But first, a down payment for "the cause" – 'as a sign of good faith you understand'. Oh, and a commitment to abide by "the rules of conspiracy", as he called them.

14

That was the catch, no meeting with Freitas was ever straightforward, because of those "rules of conspiracy". Take the Roman Cemetery – my first foray into the Old Town since my stay at the *Gatto Negro*. We needed a full moon for me to locate the gap in the perimeter wall. But moonlight has its downside. Although it would be the dead of night, there would be no cover of darkness, no protection from the uniform guarding the oak tree – a rallying point for Italian Separatists, don't ask me why. Then the next hazard: the cemetery was more a dump for unwanted sculptures – broken capitals, chipped Medusa heads, statues with lopped off limbs, monuments with carved Latin inscriptions – a pretty formidable obstacle course when you are groping your way like a blind man, stumbling and tripping over tree roots and clumps of rock.

I was beginning to suspect that the whole thing might be a giant hoax, a revolutionary's idea of a practical joke – the kind they might play on a raw recruit. But one thing you could never pin on Freitas was a sense of humour.

My instructions were to make for a Gothic rose window, lying on its side like a discarded wagon wheel. Freitas had drawn it for me in a pen and ink sketch that was as delicate as a watercolour. His memory was faultless – there was even hatching to suggest the bed of gravel filling the gaps in the tracery where there had once been stained glass. But for practical purposes a map would have been more use.

There was a peculiar menace to the place that seemed to encapsulate my fears and which I found profoundly unsettling. What I most feared were cats. Wild, ravenous vermin! After that the ghosts who walk at night, like Hamlet's father, suffering spirits trapped or imprisoned, their only pleasure in death to scare the living shit out of us mortals. Sensing movement in the shadows, I raised my walking stick and took a few tentative swings. When Freitas touched me it was as if the archaeologist Winckelmann himself, had stepped out the shadows of his tomb to accuse me of murder.

Freitas' "rules of conspiracy", I discovered, were a habit he put on and took off like that coat of his. There was the time I saw him hiding in plain sight as it were, to cover the opening of the new Fish Market. I watched him set up his tripod on the seafront. While he was adjusting the lens, a gust blew the blanket from the camera and a young boy in a sailor suit ran to pick it up. As he handed it over, they exchanged a few words before the boy ran back to his mother. I wonder now whether this trivial detail ever turned up in the records of the Austrian secret police.

Sitting on the harbour wall and munching a *crostini,* I perused (if that's the word) my second-hand copy of *Voices from the Spirit World* purchased from Schimpf's bookshop. The sea breeze played fast and loose with the pages as I speculated about the possibility of spirits transmitting messages through the medium of the Victrola I had been admiring in a shop window earlier that morning. Might it not some day be possible to develop a receiver capable of detecting the vibrations of hidden voices, operating on frequencies outside the normal human range? After all spirits have been nabbed, caught in the act as it were, in photographs. I would have liked to have asked Freitas for his opinion there and then, but the "rules of conspiracy" got in the way.

It was under the old aqueduct that he gave me the package, cautioning me not to open it until I was well out of sight. It contained press cuttings about a strike which had taken place in the shipyard ten years earlier and which, according to Freitas, were supposed to put my photograph into context. It cost me another 10 crowns, the alternative being to tell him who killed Kolya Konradi.

As he took the money, I could have sworn he said, 'He had it coming.'

15

Another memory. Freitas is sitting at the opposite end of a carriage on the cog railway, wearing blue tinted spectacles, a black broad-brimmed hat, a bright red woollen scarf tossed dramatically about his neck and what, from a distance, I take to be some kind of cloak, also black. It is a get-up that reminds me more of the theatre manager in a French cabaret poster than a secret agent.

I was thinking of Kolya and our final meeting on the Lustgarten. I tried to imagine him working a crowd, rallying a bunch of stokers and boilermakers chucking lumps of plaster at Austrian cops, sabres drawn. Was this the same Kolya? It wasn't just his threads or the gold cufflinks, or addressing the Head Waiter by his first name when he asked to see the wine list. Throw in for good measure the Villa overlooking the Tiergarten, father-in-law's banking interests in the Rhineland and St Petersburg, the Ukranian estate with its mills and vodka distilleries and you have the paradox. I remembered a chance remark he made about the Balkan crisis, then just getting into its stride: 'I hope they don't close the Straits – it'll play havoc with the price of grain.'

The carriage struggled with the gradient as it made the steep climb to the karst. Opicina was a Slovenian settlement where, Freitas had assured me we would be among friends. But instead of heading into the village, we took a side turning into woods where we tramped for a good twenty minutes before stopping at a small clearing that smelt pleasantly of pine and wood smoke. I wondered, was he been guided to the spot by the red circles painted on the trunks of particular trees? I was still pondering this when Freitas wheeled around to face me, his features distorted with rage. 'Cavorting with Jesuits now, are we?' he yelled. I glimpsed a flash of metal, then felt a jab in the hand I had raised instinctively to protect myself. He had stabbed me – *me* – with a penknife. I rammed my stick hard into his chest, catching him right on the breastbone. A palpable hit! Oh how I enjoyed watching him struggle for breath while I set about wrapping my injured hand with a handkerchief. The man really was demented. Jesuits? I had to think fast. I had a choice: cut and make a run for it, or stick with it until I found Kolya's girl. The girl won.

I waited for him to put away the knife and explain himself.

'I saw you with him yesterday afternoon in front of the church.'

The bastard had been shadowing me! He must have been in the crowd gathered outside San Antonio to read the daily bulletin on the pope's condition.

'No change, I'm afraid,' Hinteregger had said, seizing me firmly by the arm as he retreated down the steps. 'It's his heart.'

Freitas was back on his high-horse. 'Your *friend* makes it his business to pro-sel-y-tise' (he liked the word evidently) 'proselytise at the port – him and that creeping Jesus of a priest. Filling honest men's heads with Christian mumbo-jumbo Brand. Stay well clear of him if you know what's good for you.'

I discovered later that Hinteregger had had a run-in with a face in my photograph, an unpleasant braggart by the name of Nito. They were arguing over the existence of God. According to Freitas, Nito had slapped his pocket watch on the table and, thrusting out his chin, had challenged the Almighty to strike him dead in five minutes. Hinteregger had flown into a rage at the blasphemy and reported Nito to the police.

16

I thought it might be worth tracking down the café where their little band used to meet. It was only a tram ride from town, not in Theresianstadt as I had first supposed, nor in the Old Town, but in the port district of San Giacomo, at the far end of the Montuza Tunnel, engineering marvel and tourist attraction rolled into one. When I got there, I was disappointed to find little to distinguish it from the Old Town, although at least it was easier to get one's bearings. The streets ran up or downhill from the main square which was dominated by an enormous basilica, one of the few buildings not in a dilapidated state. Surely Kolya would have detested this place, the gutters choked with rubbish, the air reeking of sewage, many of the streets still unpaved and impassable to traffic of the most primitive kind. Women queued with weary resignation as they waited their turn at the water pump (there was no proper supply and the only fountain was in front of the church). Teetering on the hillside were houses crumbling from neglect while cows were left to graze on the fetid wasteland. San Giacomo's saving grace were its three monuments to hope – the co-op shop, the handsome (and spotless) Children's Hospital where I imagined Comrade Ana spending her daylight hours and the Cinema-Music Hall 'Mondiale.' I traipsed the streets looking for the boarded up tavern, now climbing with the much-needed aid of my walking stick, now almost tumbling down the

Via Industriale to the gates of the shipyard, but there was no trace.

17

All those meetings and what did I have to show for it? And I had completely lost track of how much this conspiracy nonsense was costing Hoffman. The meal too I put down as expenses. We met at Freitas' suggestion in Muggia, the nearest village beyond the bay, and quite a pretty one had it not been for the pall of smoke from the factories feeding off the port. The location, a modest *trattoria,* was "secure" Freitas had assured me, his way of saying that the owner could be trusted. Thinking to blend in, I dressed the part and arrived without collar and tie in a navy blue sailor's pullover with a roll neck, matching corduroy trousers and wearing boots instead of shoes. Freitas' eyes narrowed with disapproval (did he think I was mocking him?). He introduced me to the wife of the *padrone*, a formidable stout lady with a mottled complexion and fleshy, powerful-looking arms. She good-humouredly brought over two glasses of *Prosecco* "on the house". I toasted her health while Freitas picked up the menu. I wasn't especially hungry and spent most of the meal watching my companion go to town on meat and vegetable soup and rabbit in a wine gravy. I decided that the hollowness around his eyes was probably a case of undernourishment rather than tuberculosis.

I got straight down to business. What did he mean by "Konradi had it coming"?

He stopped eating long enough to fend off the question.

'Just an expression.'

I tried to pin him down, 'This *is* Konradi we're talking about. *Konradi* had it coming?'

But Freitas backed off, claiming he had been referring to capitalists as a class as he helped himself to another chunk of bread from the basket, this time to mop up the sauce. 'This is all news to you isn't it, class warfare?'

His mouth being full, he nodded vigorously to signal it was all right with him if I wanted to defend my ignorance. I left the field to him.

'Your problem comrade is that you are only capable of seeing things from the standpoint of a petty-bourgeois. If you had grown up among real workers, got a job in a factory, or a mill, got to know the shop floor, you'd view things differently.'

I wasn't buying in to the Marxist stuff, but I let him continue.

'You see yourself as a man of business, am I right?'

'Tradesman,' I corrected. 'I work with my hands.'

'Good – very good. But it's a matter of ownership. Your tools, and your premises come to that, are your private property. You pay wages to your staff, but you keep the profits for yourself... I rest my case. What's so funny?'

It was his habit of scratching the back of his neck while smirking with a crooked sideways twist of the lips, a mannerism of the star in *The Little Cretin Goes to the Races* and even now whenever I think of Freitas, up pops the comic character, Signore Cretinetti.

'My turn to start,' said Freitas. 'We can assume can we that Konradi was bumped off? Come off it Brand, you don't believe the official version any more than I do. Otherwise you wouldn't be here looking for the girl.'

Freitas had his own theory about the murder, that the Comrades (which comrades he didn't specify) had their doubts about Kolya from the off.

We were getting somewhere! Was it an exemplary beating he wanted to know, a warning to others. What could I tell him about the body?

'Don't be dense Brand. Was anything found on him, was there a note, a calling card?'

His theory struck me as far-fetched but it would go part of the way to explain something that had been troubling me – why Kolya's body had been found in such a remote spot and so far from the embassy. Might it be possible that he had received a message calling him away and had walked into a trap?

If I wanted to get to the truth, I needed to talk to the people in the photograph.

Freitas reaffirmed the woman with the pince-nez was Comrade Ana. According to him, she was Russian, but could have passed for an Italian, speaking the language, including the local dialect, with complete fluency. Nito had left Trieste for Italy to avoid the draft. The last Freitas had heard he was running a Socialist newspaper. Kolya's girl was called Zoya and was also hard of hearing. (No wonder Freitas was spooked when I turned up on the scene!)

Kolya was the only one to escape arrest. The others were awaiting trial when a huge crowd stormed the courtroom, demanding Ana's release because of her humanitarian work at the hospital. In the end the authorities thought it better to have the lot of them expelled.

Comrade Ana had moved to Milan, find her and I would find Kolya's girl.

.

MILAN

1

The conquering hero returns! How many times did I play out my triumphant homecoming in those long months I was away? 'Here's the thing. Working for the Konradis you get treated like royalty. These people, when they stay in hotels, they have a bathroom all to themselves – hot and cold running water, gold taps, towels pre-warmed on the radiator, the works. No more washstands and pitchers of lukewarm water for me...' that was the right tone for the regulars in *Destille* but for my interview with the *Echo* I would have to raise my game: 'Local Bike Dealer Solves Friend's Murder Single-handed'.

Now, closing my eyes, I am reliving the sensation of wallowing in a real bath, stretching my legs as far as they will go without running up against the rim. I miss the blanketing warmth, the tingle of soap bubbles as they pop and burst on the skin.

Hoffmann had booked me into a first class hotel that didn't cost me a pfennig as Kolya, or it could have been the wife's side of the family, was a major investor in the business. Not only that, the staff had been given instructions to cater for my– how did Hoffman put it? – My "special requirements". At every turn I was greeted with a "Prego signore" or "Certo signore", a consideration that puts us Berliners-with-attitude to shame.

It was in the bath that I would read through Gerda's letters. Just like mother when I was at boarding school, she wrote every two days without fail and became frantic if more than a week passed before I got around to mailing her back. Then, by return, would come the rebuke with double exclamation marks: 'Only two pages!! What kind of brother are you?' or 'you didn't answer ANY of my questions!'

She is a good letter writer, entertaining, funny, quite literary when the mood takes her. She has a knack for alternating down-to-earth newsy passages with whimsical flights of fancy that remind me of Robert Walser in *The Illustrated Weekly*. There's one passage where she describes walking to the tram stop at Hallesches Tor and having the feeling that the statues on the bridge over the canal seemed to be addressing an audience – waving, smiling, making speeches, sighing. Pure Walser! And Walser has a huge following. But when I point this out to her, her response is a caustic look that says, 'Do I seem like a lady of leisure to you?' And the subject is closed.

What Walser doesn't do is write in different coloured inks, a schoolgirl habit. Inside a paragraph, sometimes a single line, the colour might change from red to green, to mauve, to black as the mood suits. She is equally fond of doodling in the margins, caricatures of friends usually (quite witty some of them). Sometimes I wonder though: isn't this the kind of thing people do to "buck up" children in hospital?

"Guess who I saw at the magic show?" she wrote at one point. From the accompanying drawing I knew immediately she was referring to Reuss. It was a joke of ours to depict our "friend" with exaggerated Semitic features on account of his being a tight-wallet – he is no more Jewish than I am. She had placed a hookah pipe between a pair of swollen lips, from which smoke rings were emerging in multi-coloured spirals. It was Gerda who had introduced me to Reuss after they met at a concert. The magic show she was referring to was at the science theatre in the Exposition Park. One of the turns that night was Carl Willmann who I recognised from the conjuring shop on Kronenstrasse where he used to serve behind the counter. Willmann is not one of your common or garden children's party entertainers but a man of science, setting out to debunk the charlatans and fraudsters who give the study of the paranormal a bad name.

2

Coincidence? Who should come into the shop this morning but an army despatch rider, wheeling a brand new Viktoria, the self-same model I had noticed in Milan. What such a bike, made across town in Friedrichshain and fitted with Fichtel and Sachs coaster hubs for freewheel and back pedalling, was doing on the Piazza del Duomo, unlocked, propped against a lamppost and without any sign of the owner, was a mystery. Was it a phantom? Was I alone in seeing it? Or had my own psychic energy willed it into being?

I clamped the despatch rider's bike to the stand and set to work with the tire iron, pointing out to its owner that the fork and the frame were not "true". A professional rider and he hadn't even noticed! I inspected the rim tape with a magnifying glass (the light in the workshop is never as good as I would like) before showing him the little crease in the inner tube, right by one of the spoke holes. If I hadn't sorted that problem out, he'd have been back within a week, mended puncture or no.

Bernt, my apprentice, has still not learnt how to use a chamois properly and left a greasy trail of streaks and smudges which, had he painted them red or green, might have passed for modern art. I dealt with him and while I was front of shop watched the sign maker at work. I saw this was making him feel uncomfortable but

I wanted to ensure that he had spelled "agents for Fichtel und Sachs" correctly and remembered to add "also Hercules Works (motorcycles)."

3

The last thing I was expecting that day in Milan was a fog so dense that passers-by were vaporising and re-appearing like spirits passing through a wall. There was rain in the fog, the kind that pricks the cheeks and seeps into the eyes and an acrid smell that was familiar. I nailed it on returning to Berlin – lignite.

To get out of the rain more than anything – I was in no mood for sightseeing – I headed for the Duomo. There was a beadle on the door, a flunkey with a cocked hat and gold braided sleeves. I avoided eye contact as he let me through in case he was angling for a tip. There was a crush around the water stoop and when I tried to ease past, a Sister of Charity came close to poking me in the eye with the starched wing tip of her headdress.

I was already used to Catholic churches; but it was still my policy to sit at the back, fear of idolatry having been drummed into me at elementary school. The nightmares I had – statues ganging up on me the moment my back was turned! Even in Italy I would get a prickly feeling at the back of my neck after reaching a certain point in the nave and would cling to my Baedeker as if it was a sea-tire or a charm against evil spirits.

Maybe it was an inner anxiety, the desperation not to screw up, that led to doubts as to whether I was equal to the role Kolya had assigned me. Not that I lacked experience of dealing with bereaved widows; it was that usually, by the time I arrived on the scene, they were over the initial shock, more or less calm and under control if not exactly resigned. Now it was me who would be the one to break the news, the constable knocking solemnly at the front door.

It was time to listen to my breathing, to become aware of my pulse, the blood-rush. I closed my eyes and imagined a spot at the geometrical midpoint of my forehead and prepared to travel through it into a world beyond.

All I could see at first was an image of the woman in front – kneeling, her head plunged into her arms which were thrust outwards, hands locked in entreaty, as if begging for her very life. I tried again, to see if I couldn't tap into Kolya's psychic energy, to help him reach the girl Zoya with me as a sort of conduit. I wanted her to feel, ahead of our meeting, that Kolya was already enjoying *Devachan*, the state of bliss where, freed of his material self and surrounded by the auras of loved ones, he was at peace. A verse of Goethe's came to mind, the one carved on Frieda's tombstone:

"One morning you awoke no more

But the birds still sing, just as yesterday they sang.

In the course of the new day nothing alters

Only that you have gone away.

Now you are free and our tears wish you well!"

But could I count on her not having come across the lines herself in some cemetery or other, or in the obituary pages?

The more I dwelt on it, the more the situation seemed like new territory for me. What if she burst into tears, or swooned in my arms like Henny Porten in *Dance of the Apaches*? I was getting horribly worked up. I reached into my inside pocket to make sure I still had the locket. It was calming to sift the delicate threads of the chain through my fingers. Resting the little heart in the palm of my hand, I prised open the lid with my thumbnail but couldn't make out her image in the gloom.

Striking the right note was vital. "I have some bad news. Bad, or upsetting? Distressing perhaps,... tragic? Kolya is... plain dead or murdered, ... robbed and killed... beaten to a pulp in the dead of night?" No!

There was movement inside the cathedral, a service in the offing, time to go – the Latin inscriptions on the tombs of long-dead condottiere would have to wait.

The fog had begun to lift but seemed in no mood to hurry, as if it might be having second thoughts. I spotted a bar conveniently close to No. 63. It was dangerously early to stop off for a beer and chaser but I needed fortification. I went inside and asked for a *Dreher*. No *Dreher, Peroni*. Not the same, not the same at all. Then a Peroni with a *Marillenschnapps* on the side. What came was a *Sambuca*.

The glass, the bottle, the flowers reminded me of a still life – *nature morte*. But there was something missing – fruit and a fish gleaming on a platter. I made do with the sugar dispenser.

What the place needed, I don't mean the bar, but the arcade (the glass menagerie Zoya would call it), was a Panoptikon like *On-the-Lindens,* or *Carstens* on Friedrichstrasse. I could have wiled away a whole afternoon with the Secrets of the Sultan's bedchamber, or the two-headed lady from Siam, or, in the waxworks, the tableau of a beheading of a Boxer rebel; and the peepshow in the passageway, and the itinerant dirty-books' seller. Damn good value for 50 pfennigs!

I remembered a tip from Lindstrom – he had found it in one of those *How to be Successful* manuals. If you told yourself something enough times, you started to believe it. So if I said I was pumped up and ready for the off like a racing cyclist on a time trial, that is how I would feel. After all spiritual healing was my calling, had been ever since Auntie had seen me chatting to the angel on the tombstone.

4

No.63 – Tirriochi's Clothing Store and House of Fashion. I was checking my reflection in the plate glass window before going in, when I noticed a young woman stepping on to a little dais to adjust the costume on a mannequin. For an instant I thought it might be her. It wasn't of course. I made myself known and was shown to an alcove beside the hat stand. There was a leather banquette, a plant with the darkest leaves I have ever seen and a coffee table strewn with back numbers of *Ladies' Home Journal* and *Harper's Bazaar.* From this nook I had a grandstand view of the cashier, a freckly redhead with a fetching pout, perched on a high stool. I watched her as she "rang up" on one of those American nickel-plated cash registers you find in all the best department stores nowadays. They had a pet name for it, I discovered later, "Kitty". Picking up the nearest glossy from the pile, I went through the motions, faking interest while my eyes snacked on the redhead's silk-stockinged ankle which she flexed from time to time.

I imagined writing this up for Gerda: "Picture your brother on the loose in a ladies' dressmakers." And such a swish set up! For a while I was mesmerised by these young women going about their work: kneeling to adjust a hem here or measure out a bridal train there, passing down a consignment of chiffon or organdie, appraising a contour for the umpteenth time without betraying a flicker of irritation, emerging from a cubicle to fetch smelling salts (nothing like squeezing into a corset to bring on a fainting fit). It was as satisfying in its way as watching the meshing of well-oiled gears.

I checked myself again, this time in the full-length mirror. I had on my grey suit, a white shirt and a dark blue tie (so far so good) but had forgotten to have my shoes shined. I buffed them with a handkerchief when I thought no one was looking, but the scuffmarks were still visible. It was the act of bending down that first alerted me to an ominous pressure in my waterworks and it became ever more insistent the longer I was made to wait. The pain took me back to the schoolroom, squirming in my seat while the master intoned cruelly appropriate lines from Goethe's Faust.

Mephistopheles: Let me go my friend – now! Stop playing games with your affliction.

Faust: I'm not listening.

Mephistopheles: You know what will happen.

Faust: It can wait.

Mephistopheles: I'll soon be back.

He was right of course. I stood up, not quite straight, and excused myself to a sales assistant, pleading a pressing engagement. I apologised and promised to return the following day. But I had only got as far as the hat-stand when I felt a hand on my shoulder.

'Herr Brand?'

5

'I don't look a bit like Henny Porten,' Zoya said, long after that first disastrous meeting.

I wasn't thinking so much of Henny in *Dance of the Apaches*, but of her profile in a publicity photograph where she is wearing a black chiffon blouse.

'Black again. What were you expecting – a house plunged into mourning, a veiled vision in black crepe playing demurely with the folds of her dress? *Quelle folie!*'

So much for Gerda's female intuition.

'But that was ages ago.'

She meant Trieste, she meant Kolya. One let down after another. It was like standing on a stepladder while someone saws off the rungs one at a time.

I made a complete hash of telling her how Kolya had died – it would have made matters a lot easier if she had been willing to use sign language.

'You could have written and saved yourself the trouble. I can't go waving my arms about in the store.'

I was shocked. "Waving your arms about". That's how *they* talk.

'It was difficult enough getting taken on in the first place. Luckily for me, Madame Tirriochi is religious. Ana found that out. She tracked down a priest and persuaded him to put in a good word. Don't ask me how. A priest, and her a militant atheist!'

'And was it Comrade Ana who came up with the idea that I was a probate lawyer?'

'Well, you can't blame me for thinking there might be something in it for me.'

Probate lawyer wouldn't have been so bad, but a *private investigator*? It was my dress sense apparently. The jacket didn't sit well, the sleeves were too long. She could see just by looking at the cuffs that my shirt seams didn't meet at the shoulder. "Clothes maketh the man." So I was a let down. I should have expected as much because from the moment I set eyes on her, she oozed style and the view from the back as she led me upstairs! I captured it perfectly with a single mental snapshot. Was it silk or satin she had on underneath, a petticoat, like the one I had seen in Lindstrom's sample case, or a bodice with suspenders dangling? I liked the way she moved with a cool poise, a calm authority, a walk that said, "This is my domain. Here I'm in my element."

6

Zoya had touched a nerve with the "private investigator" remark. Yet, in a way she was right – investigating was exactly what I was about, or would be from now on, no less for discovering that she alone was not the answer to the riddle of that blasted box. I needed to find out more about the circumstances of Kolya's death and what lay behind it. If I lacked the necessary experience, the special aptitudes, the nouse it takes to be a "Gumshoe Fritz", well, I could learn couldn't I? I set myself a test: Could I have got a better response to the photograph? Maybe if I had claimed the girl was in danger, that would have grabbed their attention. I can almost see them in my mind's eye, the customers gathering around on tiptoe to peer over my shoulder. Then the follow-up questions – "How about him? Think back." "And the café itself? Where would they hang out do you think, if you had to put money on it?" That would have been showing what my mother called gumption.

Something told me that Zoya was still key to getting a handle on Kolya but there was more to it than that. I was missing the simple things – the smell of cooking, peeling paint on a window ledge, movement behind an open door, flowers that weren't changed every day, items of furniture that didn't go together – this was why I held onto the locket, so I would always have a reason to pay her another visit.

The first thing she did of an evening, even before taking off her coat, was to bring a steaming basin of water from the communal kitchen across the hall so she could bathe her feet in front of the fire – much like Gerda after finishing her shift at the hospital only with Zoya there was more poise, more… more polish in the way she lifted her skirts no higher than was necessary, while lowering her feet daintily into the bowl. Her toes were remarkable when you considered her line of work, never swollen and not a corn or bunion to be seen.

She surprised me one evening, breaking the silence by asking, 'What's he like, Kolya's little boy?'

There are occasions when I miss hearing an inflection in a voice. I guessed though, from the expression on her face, that what I would have picked up was a barely perceptible tremor.

'He has his father's ears,' was all I could come up with.

But she misunderstood and I had to explain that his hearing was fine. I was referring to the way they stuck out – Kolya's nickname at school was "Jug".

'And his wife?'

'Oh she hears too, perfectly well.'

'He struck out then. He always said he would marry who he liked. He was very vocal on that subject, how they wanted to push us around, stop us from breeding.' She meant the racial hygiene lobby, the eugenicists as they liked to call themselves to give their arguments a scientific air. I was reminded of something the clap doctor said. After the examination, when he was through with drying his hands, he had read me the "If you can't keep away from night-town, at least wear a rubber" lecture. I had assumed he had been warning me of the dangers of VD until he threw in for good measure: "There's no knowing how the child might turn out. Would you want that on your conscience?"

The subject of hearing came up again later when she was running the sewing machine. That was how she spent her evenings, making clothes, sometimes of her own design – variations on patterns she had seen at work or in advertisements. My job was to pass her anything that wasn't close to hand, or to look for the clothing scissors, which were 'kept' in the sewing drawer but were always going walkabout. I also came to be quite handy with a needle and thread although Gerda never got to hear about it.

I asked her whether she'd heard of the Phonophor. She took her foot off the treadle so I could explain that it was the latest in battery-powered hearing aids. Kolya's wife was keen for him to try it. She had been given a test model by a relative who worked for Siemens. Now I have it — the headphone set with a microphone and lots of wires are gathering dust because there's no one to show me how to use it. I keep my shaving tackle in the case.

Zoya said, 'One of these days they'll come up with something that will work, something small enough to fit in a handbag with an ear piece you can hide in your hair.'

'Doesn't it frighten you that one day they'll rope you into their hearing world and that will be that?'

'You mean we'll be expected to join in the conversation, no matter how boring the company?' She burst out laughing and it was as if the sun had come out.

7

She could easily have found a better flat in another part of town. But it had to be Brera, not only because it was convenient for Madame Tirriochi's, but because it was Bohemian (her word). To me Bohemian conjures up images of starving artists and feverish consumptives, of Mimi and Rodolfo. As it happened, one of Zoya's neighbours, Adolfo Hohenstein, had designed the posters for the premiere of Tosca at La Scala.

Zoya had to settle for a cramped apartment on the fourth floor, which, even then she could afford only by taking in one of the juniors as a lodger. I will always associate her place with the smell of *Solyanka*, Russian potluck, which was pretty much all she ate during the week. At home, when Baba made us *Solyanka,* it would always have a dollop of sour cream on top, but Zoya was for doing without – there was no butter or sugar in the house either and if I wanted milk with my coffee I went out for it.

I had to wait for her next payday to find out the reason for the penny pinching. She asked me to meet her at the studio of a local craftsman on Piazza San Marco. Leopardi specialised in Jugendstil, what the Italians call Style Liberty. He was never short of work as there was a call just then for Jugendstil houses in a new part of town called Porta Monforte. I was impressed (and a bit put out) watching their cosy *tete-a-tete* as they discussed the finer points of porcelain. She was there to collect a ceramic vase with a fancy pewter mounting that had a reserve notice pinned to it.

'How much did that run to?' I asked her when we got back.

'Spoken like a true Prussian shopkeeper!' She laughed, smart-Aleck-wise, while leading me by the hand into her half of the bedroom and a cupboard full of Jugendstil glasses and bowls. Standing awkwardly among them, a bronze statuette of a young girl with pinched features and shoulder-length tresses which bore an uncomfortable resemblance to the model in the Trieste photographers.

'Why hide them away?' I asked.

We took a little detour to Porta Monforte to find out. She had her eye on one of the houses there, a dream home you might say as she would never have been able to afford anything like it on her wages. One day, she explained, all those *objets d'art* would be on display in the corner apartment with the wrought iron balcony and the tile paintings of languid ladies. I came to think of it as her doll's house.

But I am being unfair. There was more than fantasy at work. I sussed a long-term goal with a plan of campaign to carry it through. Zoya ran on ambition like a motor car runs on petrol. Marriage, children, family life seemed no longer part of her calculations. She was carving out a future for herself that excluded Madame Tirriochi, a time when she would own her own store, sell her own creations. But for that she needed capital, which put her in a bind. I recalled what she said about probate lawyers and hearing something to her advantage. What she might have done with even a small bequest! Kolya had unsurprisingly been a disappointment while I was a mere shopkeeper.

It seemed a pity, I thought as I picked up the leather-bound portfolio with her Paris drawings. Zoya travelled there twice a year with 'Madame' to make the rounds of the fashion houses on Rue de la Paix and to view the models parading in the Bois de Boulogne or at Longchamps. Turning the pages, I was bowled over by these sketches, of figures viewed from front and back, torsos with a multitude of hairstyles and streamlined silhouettes, all vertical lines, triangles and diamonds. In the margins were her notes on materials and colours – taffeta, lace, shell pink, powder blue, ivory. I pointed to a silk number that might have belonged in Ancient Greece, a shift so revealing as to be almost transparent. 'Are there really women who wear dresses like that?' I wondered aloud.

The technique they used to get this effect, Zoya explained, was called 'cutting on the bias'.

'Look at me,' she said, placing one leg over the other and leaning back in her chair, 'and tell me what you notice.' She took my hands and placed them on her hips and pelvis. 'Feel the way my dress follows the contours of my body – see?'

No corset. No more whalebone, no more being trussed up. In future women would dress as they pleased, to hell with what men wanted. The gospel according to Zoya.

'You can take your hands away now.'

She was on to something, I realise that now. Take the hobble skirt, dreamed up according to Zoya just so European women could shuffle around like Japanese geishas and give us chaps a thrill. Hobble skirts have come and gone but what about silk stockings, rising hemlines? Isn't the latest fashion always about pleasing men? Now they've come up with a uniform designed especially for women volunteering for the Red Cross: 'smart, efficient...ladylike.'

Interesting – back in the '90s hearties and athletic types thought nothing of ditching their tailcoats and baggy trousers for more practical outfits when out cycling, but when women dared to show up in culottes they were jeered at or dismissed as "hags" or "tarts".

Culottes come into a recurring dream I have about Frieda. We are in a field with other members of our cycling club, the Dynamos, on a Sunday outing when we get into an argument with a bunch of farm hands who are blocking our path and taunting Frieda on account of her culottes. We all get so caught up in this petty dispute, that no one else notices a tram approaching. I see it getting closer but when I warn them, no one takes any notice. Until, at the last moment, when the car is nearly on top of us, the crowd bifurcates, like a divided skirt. But Frieda, who has now changed her culottes for a petticoat, has snagged the hem on the back wheel of her bicycle and cannot move.

8

Make no bones about it, going out with a woman like Zoya on your arm was a bit like riding the Luna Park roller coaster – terrific, but white-knuckle terrifying when she was in a mood to stand on her principles. I'm thinking of an afternoon in the English Gardens. There she was looking a picture, adjusting her hat with a gloved hand (her "Sunday" hat with the fruit on top, very fashionable that year), a gesture that looked natural although I now suspect it had been rehearsed many times in front of a mirror. Then out of the blue: 'Look at that woman over there – her blouse is such a tight fit around the arms that she won't be able to move her knife and fork. That's exactly what I meant by "fashion dupe" but she can't see it.'

She had raised her voice and people were staring. She was making a scene. But why? To make a point, or to make mischief? With Zoya you could never be sure, but what a blast!

For our night out at the Eden she had changed her hairstyle to a "Maria Stuart", wearing it in a kind of wreath, swept up from the neck onto the top of her head. Her hair was not black or smoky-blue as I had imagined but auburn, with an aura that reminded me of autumn leaves. She was modelling a shimmering, black, silk evening gown for Madame, low-cut and warn with a belt, inspired, she said, by the Spring collection of a Paris fashion house. Madame also chose her perfume — currently *Infini* by Caron. The effect was sensational.

The Café Eden — *Il "meet" del pubblico Milanese* — had been her idea. Leaving me with the programme, she had rested a hand lightly on my shoulder, in a gesture that suggested it might be fun. The Palace of Varieties took up an entire block below the Castello Sforza and was purpose built. According to the leaflet the attractions included roof terrace, Bier Keller, billiard room and skating rink. You could pay just for the show but I reckoned it would work out cheaper to go for the "dinner included" package.

We were between acts and on our third glass of Asti when she said, 'Tipsy already?'

I replied with the sweep of an arm that took in the gleaming cutlery, the gilded marble pilasters, the ceiling frescos, the glass dome... I had never serenaded a woman in my life but, at that moment, I felt an irresistible urge to launch into Mignon's song about Italy (lyrics only):

'Do you know the land where the lemon-trees grow,

Among darkened leaves gold oranges glow.'

She smiled. 'So you're staying?'

I had been fretting about overheads, the competition from

Fahrrad Frank's, the pressing need for a business plan (the boom years were over).

'Then I'll need help with Hoffmann.'

Stroking the lapels of my dinner jacket she said, 'Tell him... Tell him I'm a discarded mistress of Kolya's who's down on my luck and needs a loan to tie me over. Come on Theo! It's a win at the races – an opportunity to make something of yourself. Look at the improvement already, and we've hardly started. *Carpe Diem?'*

'Buyer beware?'

'Seize the day!'

'Alright, I give up. Does this mean anything to you?'

I wanted to ask her about an item from Kolya's box, the medal. I took it from my pocket and held it up by its scarlet ribbon. The bar was adjustable so it could be worn around the neck.

She showed me how by placing it carefully over my head.

It was the Russian inscription on the back I wanted translated.

'It means for "Zeal" – services rendered.'

Services for what? As far as I knew Kolya had never been in the Army.

'It may not have been his. It may have belonged to his father, or another relative. Or there's a military connection we don't know about.'

But I never got any further because at that point the compere returned to the stage. We consulted the programme: we'd done the circus act, the troupe of Serbian dancers, and the patriotic *mise en scene* involving real soldiers from the Italian army. Next up was 'The world's strongest man', billed as having been brought direct from the Folies Bergeres. By rights I should have felt short-changed, as I knew for a fact that the title belonged to a German, Sandow whereas this Hercules or whatever his stage name was, came from Denmark. His warm-up routines with the weights impressed Zoya I could tell. Finally a cannon was wheeled onto the stage. We watched a diminutive negro insert the ball, then stand back to light the fuse. Zoya made a grab for my hand as Hercules stood directly in the line of fire only feet away. The floor shook, smoke billowed from the barrel and there was Hercules clutching the ball to his chest.

9

I sometimes lie awake thinking about her and Kolya, from their first meeting in Pirano, the resort on the Austrian Riviera, to the time of her arrest when Kolya uncoupled himself like a wagon getting gradually left behind by a goods train. She had finger spelled Pirano for me so there would be no further misunderstanding: 'As if Kolya would wait in line in the Pirona patisserie.'

A day out with "the girls." Shop girls, fellow socialists? They are walking the walls when she stops to take a photograph. She had a camera? She had never mentioned that before.

'My camera, a friend's, what does it matter?'

She drops a glove onto the ledge below. Then, bang on cue, who should show up but Kolya, with his chum from the Commercial School, the Austrian cadet. They try retrieving the glove with a stick, then commandeer a fishing rod, but it is still out of reach. Zoya protests but they insist on persevering. Kolya asks for a forwarding address for the glove. A week or so later it arrives, with a message and a bunch of flowers. Kolya Konradi a gallant?

At that point I fall asleep and by the morning it no longer seems important.

10

How is it that, with everyone I meet or try to get to know, I end up confiding something I regret — nothing of importance, a shortcoming, a foible, but personal; then to have it thrown back in my face. Why, in an unguarded moment did I confess to Zoya, albeit in a light-hearted, jesting sort of way, the reason I had never taken up smoking? — In case I was asked for a light at a party and didn't catch on quick enough.

"Smokes." Cigarettes were always "smokes" with Zoya. As in "Where are my smokes?" or "What have I done with my smokes?" If you are going to use slang, what's wrong with down-to-earth expressions, "ciggie" or "fag"?

Our first serious argument: a woman's right to smoke in a public place.

We are crossing Via Manzoni on the way to the Academy when she turns back at the kerb to "cadge a light" (another of her expressions) from a passer by. When she finally catches up and tries to take my arm, I shrug myself free.

How many times had I begged her not to smoke on the street? Even in *dolce-far-niente*-land it drew stares, disapproving looks, the wrong kind of attention. But Zoya was as difficult to budge as a window that won't open because the catch has been painted over.

She gives the mock salute. *'Jah-wohl.'* She is speaking at the top of her voice (perhaps without realising it) and people are giving her funny looks. Is she slurring her vowels, or drawling in a way that sounds affected?

'Don't forget the goose step.' I say, taking a deep breath and digging my nails into the palms of my hands, because it's not as if she is the campaigning sort, the kind of feminist who dresses as a man or chains herself to railings...

I try changing the subject but make a mess of pronouncing the Sforza in Castello Sforza and give up. We walk the next couple of blocks in a simmering silence.

Then: 'Did I tell you, I want to learn to drive?'

'Drive?' She had spurned my offer of cycling lessons (and the chance to put my arm around her waist). 'You can't ride a bike and now you want to drive? What if you were to get oil on your clothes? What would Madame say? I'm only being practical. Women like you don't like getting their hands dirty.'

I dived into my fury, to a depth where she couldn't follow me and wallowed about. The whole Brera thing "Bohemian", "cachet" and the rest, was getting under my skin.

We took it out on the picture gallery – "doing" the crucifixions, the Madonnas with and without child, the martyrdoms, the subjects from mythology, side-on portraits of Renaissance princes, the bowls of gleaming fruit at breakneck speed, in total silence and not always together. At one point we passed one another on a staircase without so much as a nod, at another I was standing alone in the grey humourless cloister (the building had once belonged to the Jesuits) while Zoya looked down from the balustrade of an upper storey, a cigarette dangling provocatively from her lips.

We were standing in front of *The Kiss* when she started up again.

'Don't hold me back is all I'm asking.'

The Kiss always attracted a crowd for the hidden meaning, something to do with the *Risorgimento,* so I drew her away before having one last try at lowering the temperature.

'All I'm saying is, you know, that it creates the wrong impression.'

'Smoking again, *mio Dio...*'

I sensed disaster but blundered on. 'It gives some men the idea that a woman is...' I had been about to say loose... 'you know, easy-going.'

She delivered a stinging slap that brought tears to my eyes. I never raised the subject again.

11

What I first mistook to be the rumble of the tram in my recurring Frieda dream, turned out, on surfacing, to be the heel of Zoya's shoe tapping a tattoo on the night table. She had stripped the bed and appeared to be pulling off my trousers and wrestling me out of my shirt at the same time. I wanted to explain that there was puke in the waste paper basket too, but the words wouldn't come. It had been a mistake getting stuck into the *Risotto alla Milanese* with such gusto!

Now down to my Long Johns and flannel vest, I grabbed a blanket (matted with vomit) and padded across the room to the balcony where the marble floor felt deliciously cool underfoot. More than anything I would have liked to lie down where I was and close my eyes, only my impressions of the previous evening were jumping about like a film with some of the key frames missing. Convinced that I might have been guilty of something that I would later have cause to regret, I broke into a sweat. This was my first Saturday night since being signed-off by the doctor and I had decided to treat myself. Up popped the image of a tart, with a lazy eye and dark curly hair, yawning into my shoulder because I was having trouble getting it up. I had planned a sortie on the waterfront taverns of the Vicolo de Lavandai where the more presentable of the laundresses, keen to make a bit of pin money on the side, were said to hang out after work.

Just then I felt Zoya ease the soiled blanket from my shoulders and replace it with my overcoat. The tenderness of the gesture took me by surprise until on returning indoors I realised that she had stumbled on my peace offering. It was to have been flowers or another trip to the theatre, but then I thought of Leopardi's and came away with a vase which he assured me was Style Liberty.

I picked the alarm clock up from the floor and wondered how on earth I had got by so far without Strammer Max wriggling from under the blankets to lick my face until I showed signs of life.

Twelve thirty! Now I understood why Zoya was there. I was meant to be escorting her around a rival store, feigning interest while she spied for Madame.

First I had to shave. She followed me into the bathroom to watch because shaving reminded her of her father: the last memory she had of him before he disappeared from her life for good, he was lathering her face with shaving soap as a joke. He had left to go back to Russia where at some point he had got mixed up in a plot to assassinate a General. Zoya never talked about her mother. As I understood it, Comrade Ana had taken her under her wing, bringing her to Switzerland where they set up house together like a regular family. Before that, from what I could gather, it had been a pillar to post existence.

She said, 'Is this the photograph?' and produced it from behind her back, holding it over my left shoulder so I could see in the mirror. I should have been pleased that she was taking an interest but I wasn't, I was annoyed. Turning things over as she moved about a room was an irritating habit of hers, although it was careless of me to leave it lying around.

I asked her how Kolya had been able to get hold of a print when, according to Freitas, the film had been confiscated by the police.

She didn't like talking about Kolya as a rule – I guessed her curiosity had finally got the better of her. 'Kolya hadn't wanted his picture taken.'

The photograph had been Nito's idea, a way of promoting their little band. From the cuttings Freitas had given me, my impression of the strike was that it had ended badly, disastrously even. People had been killed. Yet he himself had referred to it once as a work of art – I remember because he used the German word *Kunstwerk*. Whatever the outcome of the strike, I found it hard to reconcile the image of Kolya in alpaca suit and kid boots with chopping up furniture for a makeshift barricade. But when Zoya called him their Mycaenas, in the sense that he bankrolled their activities, I realised I was on the wrong track.

It wasn't the cause he had been interested in so much as testing a theory. One day he came back from the Commercial School pumped up and out of breath. Things were hotting up he said. He'd heard rumours about secret meetings between Italians and Slovenians. There was talk of forming a united front of separatists and workers, of giving the Austrians a damned good hiding.

'We started going to meetings to observe the reactions of the strikers to individual speakers. Kolya had been reading a book about crowd psychology, how people behave in situations where emotions are running high. A tremendous energy builds up, a kind of indignation, and at some point the individual loses his sense of identity and gets caught up in the will of the collective.'

Was this, I wondered, what famous orators from the past, the Marc Anthonys and Ciceros, played on? I imagined these speechifiers as versions of Lothario or Don Juan, old hands at seduction, probing the defences of untested novices.

'We had to walk because the trams weren't running. There were demonstrations and marches where everyone linked arms and it felt like we were welded together, like links in a chain. It's true you know, you lose yourself, something takes over.'

This was after martial law was declared.

'On the first day of the emergency, there were troops lined up across the Corso to protect the businesses of Theresianstadt. We were walking arm in arm behind the banners, singing at the tops of our voices.' (They were both tone deaf.)

They held their ground until they heard shooting and had to take cover. They were being shot at! 'There was a stampede, people were screaming. I picked up a stone and was ready to throw it when Kolya pulled me away. The strange thing was that when we finally got home we couldn't wait for the action to begin again. We lay awake all that night talking things over.'

12

Zoya's hand on my thigh, higher...I reached over to return the favour but she fended me off. The hand returned, her hand in mine – a subterfuge. She really was very good, adept even with fly buttons, which, God knows can be frustrating. I cast a furtive glance at the two empty seats at the end of the row – I wasn't sure what the Dumont's policy was with latecomers, whether they let them in after the show started. If they did and the usherette appeared with a torch we would be undone in more ways than one!

The Dumont rather than the Volta, where there had been a riot during Holy Week when the newsreel was replaced by "The Way of the Cross" and the atheists in the audience began hurling sweets at the screen and the indignant believers.

We were watching *Dante's Inferno*. While Zoya went about her business, I tried to focus on the captions. On screen the adulterous lovers, Paolo and Francesca, surrounded by dozens of scantily-clad bodies – some of them stark naked – were floating like shoals of fish. Zoya was watching me in the dark, scrutinising my "El Greco look" as she called it when my face went into spasm in response to her groping. I fished in my pocket for my hankie...

I had been put out by Zoya's account of the strike. Why? I couldn't say at first, only that Kolya's behaviour seemed out of character; but then how well did I really know him? – Hardly at all. There was nothing particularly shocking about it. They went to meetings together, they linked arms, they sang workers' songs at the tops of their voices, they lay awake at night, unable to sleep for excitement, in anticipation of the events of the coming day. Smoking probably.

Then I understood – it was that Kolya was in the driving seat as it were. The book had spurred him on, jolted him into action and Zoya had been happy to follow, Zoya who with me was so certain of herself, so doctrinaire, so obdurate. And that was only what she chose to tell me about their time together. I pictured them in a carriage, her head lolling against his shoulder while she dozed. The image made me queasy, set off a fluttering in the chest that was most unpleasant and perhaps it was this sensation that galvanised me into action. I set about devising a business proposition for her: "Cycles and accessories for ladies". We would sell bloomers, divided three-quarter-length skirts, cutaway jackets, leggings, wind-resistant hats, bonnets, berets, gaiters, elegant but practical footwear. The clothes would be designed by Zoya ("formerly of Tiriocchi's in Milan") while I concentrated on operating costs, payroll, taxes, insurance – the business end of things. The smell of rubber was the main problem. Flowers were not the solution, the scent would not be powerful enough. Joss sticks, perhaps?   Of course it wasn't really a plan and I never dared tell her about it.

13

Whenever I mentioned Kolya she avoided looking me directly in the eye. That was something I had noticed and strangely it was precisely at those moments that her looks seemed to desert her. I think it was her mouth that was on the small side, giving her a slightly disgruntled, put-out expression.

I was reminded of this when I brought out Kolya's box, laying out the items in front of her without comment in the hope that she would shed more light on the strange bequest. She ignored the black mourning ribbon I had seen Kolya wearing in his lapel as a child in memory of the fallen Tsar, turned over a gold commemorative coin without comment, but seized on an empty perfume bottle with a glass stopper.

'Jasmine?' she suggested.

'Is that all you can tell from it?'

She had moved on to a postcard from Rome with Cyrillic writing.

'Now here is something. She says that she's missing him terribly…. "returning at the end of the month" …Signed P.'

'Russian girls' names beginning with a P?' I asked. It was surprisingly difficult; Zoya could come up with only two – Pelegaya and Polina. I favoured Polina.

Zoya said, 'Perhaps the music box was hers too.'

She was about to hand the card back when I pointed to the postmark (1887) and reminded her that even if it was another love interest, Kolya would have been in his teens, so she was hardly a rival.

Zoya's reaction took me aback. 'I'm not at all surprised at there being other women, "eligible" doesn't begin to describe him.'

Well, that put me in my place. I hit back.

'You mean his money.'

'There was more to him than that. He had substance, hidden depths. Even his travels... imagine visiting Bukhara and Samarkand...'

14

She emerged from the bath in a cloud of steam, wearing only a kimono. She removed the towel from her head and shook out her hair, which seemed much shorter without the extensions though the curls were her own. She may have said something as she approached the bed where I lay waiting for her, but I had eyes only for her breasts, pale globes half concealed in the folds of her gown. I wondered if I could ask her, if I dared ask her to model lacy underwear for me like Lindstrom's girl, invite her to take a turn about the room.

She was good at it. They were daring, the things she did; or rather the way she made them seem, as if she was inventing them or trying them out for the first time, as if no one else had thought of them. She reminded me of a barefoot dancer improvising at a rehearsal, stopping occasionally to ponder the next move.

'*Infini?*' I murmured, breathing her in as she climbed on top of me so that I felt the cool touch of satin on my skin. Things I had only read in pulp novels – trembling eyelashes, parted lips, thrilling under-caresses, fingers sensitive and passionate, flesh supple like the rising and curving surf – now made real. I had not expected the ostrich feather, which she worked on me until I let rip, '*Schlamper*! Bitch! Screw you!' Did she make me say the things or did the words just come out?

I wondered where these moves of hers, her conjurer's repertoire, came from. There was a period in her life, in her childhood it must have been, when she lived in a "commune", a social experiment based on the theories of some French thinker or other where I imagined she'd been allowed to run wild. If this was what they called free love, then I was all for it. Compared to what Zoya was offering, my own sexual adventures to date had been a let down. Basically sex amounted to little more than an endless succession of business transactions unless you counted the occasional knee trembler with a shop girl. Even the more accommodating of my bereaved ladies had already paid me for a consultation. With Zoya, on the other hand, sex was an innocent form of recreation given free of charge, with nothing expected in return – none of that "Can this be love?" palaver or "Where do we stand?".

'You're not listening to me.' She was laughing, resting on her elbow while she rummaged in her make up bag. 'I think I'll give you the Nijinsky look. All we need is a dab of rouge to highlight your cheekbones...' I felt the tickle of a light brush on my skin. '...and a little kohl. I know women who would kill for those eyelashes.'

When she had done, she showed me the results in the little mirror of her compact. I found them disturbing. I looked like an oversized doll, or the female impersonator, Bobby Waldon.

She read the distaste in my face and, giving up on me, got out of bed again to blow the smoke from her cigarette out of the bathroom window.

15

Is that what I was becoming, her plaything, one of those tailor's dummies? "Make something of yourself" – I barely knew who I was any more.

There was a day when it was raining heavily and we found ourselves cooped up in the hotel. I had gone down to the lobby to buy a newspaper and pick up the post. When I got back, it was to find Zoya sharing a cigarette with the maid while demonstrating a more effective way to use the trouser press. Zoya had been making herself increasingly at home, bringing with each successive visit another possession from her digs in Brera – a hairbrush, a reel of cotton, a nail file, a scent bottle. These she would leave lying about like a dog marking out its territory or an explorer planting a flag at the South Pole. I padded over to my favourite armchair to read, only to find the cushion missing. Cushions. She was in the habit of picking them up as she passed, hugging them to her bosom before discarding them wherever she happened to end up. They were talking about me: What did Eleonara (she and the maid were on first name terms) think about me growing a beard? Zoya was convinced that without whiskers Hoffman would not take me seriously. (What had happened to the Nijinsky look?). They must have discussed the facial hair of every crowned head in Europe – Nicky ('not bad') the Kaiser ('arrogant') Victor Emmanuel ('don't be ridiculous') – not to mention artists, musicians and the man who advertises safety razors in the newspapers ('Say goodbye to stropping!').

No-one thought to ask me what I wanted. Even Gerda was making decisions for me: "Hans asked me to remind you that the cycling dinner's in a month's time and I said you'd be sure not to miss it," she wrote.

Easter had come and gone, time was passing, events were moving on, new developments by the day. The newsreels were showing flickering images of the pope on the mend, of the siege of Scutari coming to a bloody close, of Italian troops flushing out Libyan tribesmen from their mountain hideouts. The skyline of Constantinople jerked into view, warships at anchor in the Sea of Marmara. If you were still with us Kolya, you would have been fretting about the threat to shipping in the Straits, the impact on grain exports.

Finally, I made up my mind. It was high time I left for Rome to confront the scene of Kolya's murder, but before that I had to report to Hoffmann.

ROME

1

In Tivoli breakfast was served on the roof terrace, from where there were terrific views of the Gorge. It was unusually warm for the time of year and to shade himself from the early morning sunlight, Hoffmann was wearing a collapsible white linen hat, rather like a cardinal's, tied under the neck with a ribbon. His ginger hair had matted around his pale forehead, which was, like the rest of his freckled skin, sheened with perspiration. Set before him were assorted hams, eggs, cheeses and caraway seed rolls. Because he talked often and at length, the food he had speared with his fork would remain suspended in mid-air for up to half a minute at a time. When the moment came to dispose of it, he chewed quickly and impatiently, anxious that anyone else might break into the conversation before he had moved on to his next point.

The Hoffmanns lived in a converted watchtower, built in the 13th century for a nobleman from the Romagna who wanted to protect his property from marauding mercenaries. The first thing they had to do before moving in, there being no inside staircase, was to build one and this spiral staircase (in keeping with the style of the period, Hoffmann maintained) now connected the three floors of the house.

The side extension had been added at a later date, but in the same Gothic style and had it not been for the climbing ivy (which admittedly gave the place a Romantic air) would have passed for authentic. Inside the original stone arches, oak beams, terracotta floors and at least two stone fireplaces had survived. I was for keeping them, but they did not fit in with Hoffmann's plans and were destined for Berlin where he was an assistant to Professor Friedländer at the Kaiser-Friedrich Gallery. A leading authority on Renaissance painting, he was in Italy to persuade hard-up Italian noblemen to part with their Old Masters. He had a colossal amount to spend; and the Kaiser was even prepared to raid the Hohenzollern coffers when the need arose. The main competition came from American tycoons like the late J.P. Morgan, whose own art collection had been estimated, according to Hoffmann, at 60 million dollars. These Yankee Mycaenases (to borrow Zoya's term) had a keen eye to business but were often ignorant when it came to artistic matters and relied on the advice of experts, not all of whom were as scrupulous as Hoffmann. There was a Mrs Gardener from Boston for instance who had been persuaded to buy what she was assured was a Titian only to find out that it was a copy made by one of his assistants. 'Though she does have some very fine things. And to be fair to her, several rooms have been fitted out splendidly and with impeccable taste.'

That must have been the morning Hoffmann went to see the Verrochio. He had invited me to come along and I was on the point of accepting – since it belonged to a genuine prince, who numbered popes and even Roman emperors among his ancestors – when I felt the pressure of Claudia's hand on my wrist. 'Or you *could* stay here.'

And so it began, with the pair of us watching Hoffmann setting off for the countryside in his chauffeur-driven car.

I wrote about Claudia in a letter to Zoya:

His wife is quite strange to look at – very pale, with hair so blonde as to be almost white and with eyebrows to match. She could easily be taken for a Dane but they're German, with Jewish blood to boot (nee Mayer or Meyer). She rubs cream into her skin to keep off the sun and so the overall effect is quite ghoulish. I now divide women into "corset-wearers" and "non". Claudia Hoffmann belongs to the first category although she has no more need of stays than I have. Maybe you could put her right on this and explain the advantages of – what was it, the "new silhouette" (?) You see, I do remember some of the things I'm told.

I didn't let on to Zoya about Claudia's idiosyncrasies in the love-making department: I didn't ever get to see her naked, and when we lay on, rather than in, the bed, it was in such a way that only our toes touched. Another thing – she didn't like being kissed on the mouth, offering her throat and neck instead to be nibbled or sucked and I was only allowed to touch her breasts if I brushed the nipples with the backs of my fingers.

2

I took advantage of Hoffman's absence to nosey around. The decoration in some of the rooms, including his study, was inspired by works of art. In the Holbein room I came across a sales catalogue from America advertising farm machinery. I was intrigued to find Kolya's name written on the inside cover. There were notes in the margin I couldn't read, as the Russian was too difficult and the handwriting too small. He'd marked various implements that specially interested him – a make of tractor and a crop-spraying machine. On a whim I decided to take it with me. In my own room I found a small bottle of scent, by coincidence *Infini* by Caron. I had assumed it belonged to Claudia until I noticed that she didn't wear perfume. Perhaps it belonged to Kolya's widow.

I was shown the rest of the house by Claudia – the well, now dry and filled with stones, the still-to-be-refurbished Gothic chapel and the outside staircase used by the servants to bring up meals from the kitchen. Finally, we explored, as far as we were able, the blocked-off secret passage from the cellar which smelt of the dessert wines stored in leaky casks along a wall and something else – it could have been musk. Claudia, touching my wrist in such a confiding way at breakfast, had left behind a strange tingling sensation which agitated me to the point where I had already given in to my urges after taking a peak at the studio photographs of the girl in Trieste. Now, the confined space, where arms, elbows and fingertips touched as if by accident, was an open invitation to intimacy. But when I made my move, she put herself just out of reach.

This was the game she liked to play: in the quiet hour after lunch, I would go looking for her in a version of hide-and-seek, while keeping up the fiction that when we did meet on the stairs, by an open door, or in the pergola it was by chance. She would arrange it so that she had her back to me and, as I crept up on her, she would turn her neck towards me and I would nibble away, getting purchase by holding on to her bony shoulders. It was like a ritual dance between particularly clumsy birds. 'Here,' she would say or 'Like this.' She could get quite shirty if you got it wrong, going as far as seizing you by the hand or even the head and directing it to the place.

'How was your day?' Hoffmann asked when he returned from work. 'Claudia's perked up since you've been here, I must say. Showing visitors around gives her something to do.'

I gave a selective and partly truthful account of our tour of Hadrian's Villa (what was left of it), translating stunted columns and slabs of marble into temples, baths and palaces. What I could not get out of my mind was the memory of Hoffmann's wife nuzzling her cheek on my shoulder, after I had followed her into the long shadow cast by a brick vault.

'When you get back to Berlin, I suggest you take a look at our own copy of Antinous.' He was turning over a figurine of a young man, completely naked, one arm raised casually to adjust his braided hair.

'Antinous,' he said. 'You've just been to the site of his last resting place. There's a rather beautiful legend about how he came to be honoured as a god after his death. Kolya was very taken by it.'

3

I could have sworn it used to hang above the glass door divide between the Konditorei and the café sitting room. The sign I mean: Baumkuchen By Royal Appointment. Now it has been moved to the wall behind the counter to make way for a large portrait of the Kaiser, dressed in full regimental uniform and with the martial bearing befitting a Commander in Chief. It's his recommendation that we should eat carrot cake: "Help the war effort – conserve butter, sugar and milk!"

Now in wartime Berlin, where even ersatz bread is rationed, I would happily sell my grannie for a crusty loaf with real tomato paste and a bowl of green olives. I spot a discarded copy of the Morning Post lying on the adjoining table and trouble my neighbour for it. He passes it across without comment, though I can guess what he is thinking: 'Shouldn't you be…?' I regret now shaving off my beard as it makes me look younger and still fit for active service.

An advertisement on the front page catches my eye: 'German Corsets for German Women, five per cent of total sales this week to go to the Red Cross.'

I think of Zoya, not for the first time – "Berlin has all the best cafes, *nicht wahr?*"

Falkenhayn I see is attributing our recent successes to the use of poison gas which drifts towards the enemy in wreathes, like soot wafting from the factory chimney on the far side of the bridge, choking the roses in the garden with a coating of soot. I think of Frank and Gunther who joined up on the same day and are now doing their bit in Flanders. I got a letter from them back in November, at least that was the date on the postmark.

The Kaiser's portrait takes me back to Bertorelli's restaurant in Tivoli where his photograph appeared alongside other celebrity visitors – only then he was dressed in civilian clothes and smiling merrily at the camera, the *Reise-Kaiser* on tour so to speak.

4

It had been Hoffmann's suggestion that she take me out to lunch. I worked up an appetite exploring the lower reaches of the famous gorge, slipping and sliding on the rough track as it followed the meandering course of the Aniene. I enjoyed myself enormously but by the time I got to the restaurant I was a bit dishevelled – collar loose, tie horribly askew, shoes and trouser cuffs caked with mud. Stopping to make myself presentable cost time and, as I feared, Claudia had beaten me to it and was standing in line for a table with a view. She was holding a book under her arm I noticed, but not the one I had loaned her: *Atlantis,* Hauptmann's latest, in which a doctor crosses the Atlantic on a passenger liner to care for his ailing wife, when the ship strikes an object in mid-ocean and sinks with great loss of life. It came out only months before the Titanic disaster and I had bought it in Trieste after reading that Hauptmann had won the Nobel Prize. It so happened that a cousin of Hoffmann had been due to sail on the fatal voyage but missed his connection and ended up travelling with the Hamburg-America line. The subject came up at dinner one evening and afterwards Claudia asked to borrow the book.

Now that we were seated, I asked her how she was getting on with it. She was fanning herself frantically, although there was hardly any need, it being April still and not July.

'*Atlantis*? I couldn't get into it.'

Just then a party of four was shown to a table under the canvas awning.

'That should have been us,' she complained, visibly peeved.

I suggested moving indoors but she wouldn't hear of it. To pass the time I returned to the subject of *Atlantis*. Didn't she think the similarities with the Titanic were uncanny? 'You have to hand it to him, the odds on that happening in real life are a million to one.'

'Couldn't it be just coincidence?'

She was wearing a colour that suited her, cornflower blue. But something about her outfit wasn't right – the hatband on the toque, or the dress itself – a fussy number with a high laced neck, long sleeves and a ragged bodice that drew unwarranted attention to her bosom. Being out in the sun was making her fret. I tried to catch the headwaiter's eye.

'You don't believe in premonitions?'

'No, frankly. There weren't enough lifeboats on the Titanic. Is that in *Atlantis*?'

I ordered a Campari and soda. Claudia was drinking orange juice but it wasn't sweet enough. I went to fetch the sugar and came back with two menus. She left hers where it was, unopened.

'What's the matter, aren't you hungry?'

'I'm dieting.'

Pulses were the thing, according to the English faddist doctor whose advice she was following, meat and fish strictly out of bounds.

'Besides it's *tavola calda,*' she explained wearily. 'You serve yourself.'

I shrugged and joined the other diners who were poring over an amazing array of dishes arranged on silver platters. I was famished and while the prospect of a meal consisting wholly of finger food was a disappointment at first, once I realised that you could keep coming back for more I began to see the advantages. The first time around I opted for the spinach ricotta, the stuffed artichokes and the salted cod. While I was making my selection I took a surreptitious glance in Claudia's direction. She had put down her fan and her book lay open in front of her but she was not reading. Something was on her mind, clearly, but what? Not my problem I decided, breaking the top off a cold beer. If she wants to tell me she will.

Eating alone is one thing, eating alone and in company quite another. It's akin to being put in the wrong through no fault of your own. It puts you off your stride.

'So what *is* it you're reading?' I asked, hoping to coax a smile. Dante. She hadn't stinted herself either, it was a leather-bound deluxe edition with marbled end-pages, part of a set, the kind you use a paper-cutter to open.

'Dante,' I said, whistling appreciatively, 'that's aiming high.'

She blushed easily. 'Not really, it's Streckfuss' parallel translation. We've got to the part about Paolo and Francesca.'

'So I see.' "We", so that was it. She had been for a confab with her priest friend. One time early in the morning I had observed her from my bedroom window, wearing a mantilla and carrying what I took to be a prayer book. I later discovered she was taking instruction in the Catholic faith, or toying with the idea at any rate.

I was admiring the illustrations when I came across a passage marked in pencil – lines about flocks of starlings being blown about in a gale.

'So that's what they were meant to be – the floating bodies, the lost souls. In the film!'

I explained about my trip to Kino Dumont, leaving out Zoya

although running through my mind was my own private reel where her fingers were deftly working my crotch. Claudia was not a cinema-goer and had not heard of *Inferno*. Fine by me.

I picked up my fork and attacked the cod.

Starlings though, why bring them in to the story? Bats I could understand. But that was the medieval mind for you, all over the place. Take Hieronymus Bosch, his paintings were teeming with goblins and demons. No starlings, though. I'd been wondering about Dante, as it happened. There was something childish it seemed to me, cruel too, about condemning your enemies to perpetual torment out of spite. And it didn't end there. Even the Ancients – Plato, Aristotle and the rest – were condemned to live through eternity as 'shades' shut out from paradise. Just for being born at the wrong time.

'The Divine Comedy,' I said thinking aloud. 'What's so comic about it?' She couldn't say. Zoya would have known.

'Why are they in hell – Paolo and Francesca,' she said removing the book from the table. You have to imagine them sitting side by side in a bower, reading about Lancelot and Guinevere. All Dante says is: "They set the book aside" That was when it happened, the occasion of sin.'

'The occasion of what?'

'Sin. After the first kiss, there can be no going back. They throw it all away – the prospect of eternal happiness gone in an instant – and all for the sake of a moment's gratification.'

It was the priest talking.

'I thought it was a poem? Then don't make it sound like a religious treatise.'

'Why can't it be both?'

My God! It explained the whole thing – our relations, everything fell into place. The way she saw it we were teetering on the edge of a precipice but without ever taking the fatal step, that first kiss on the mouth. And, by encouraging me to make all the running, she was let off the hook, convinced even that she was offering a kind of passive resistance. I shuddered inwardly at the morbidly unhealthy implications.

It could be that she had got Dante all wrong. Couldn't it be that what he was really doing, albeit on the sly, was taking a sly swipe at the theologians, insinuating that if you take their logic to its conclusion, then God is plain cruel – a despot a tin-pot tyrant?

'You have to be a Catholic to understand,' was all she said, fingering the rose pinned to her bodice.

'What's wrong?'

'This... What we're doing – it's wrong, sinful.'

I allowed her to deliver her little speech without interruption. She respected Hoffmann, it was just that she was lonely and he was away so often. What happened between us had been a mistake. Besides, there was Freddie to consider. At least she was dry-eyed.

'In any case,' I said, 'I'll be gone in a week or so...'

'Well if that's all it means to you... Still you're not to blame. You can't help it.'

'What?'

'It doesn't matter.'

'It does matter. Say what you want to say.'

'Alright then, your urges. Yes, yes all men have them, God knows, but people with your handicap can't...'

It was the way that she said it. I laughed so hard I had to cover my mouth with my napkin.

'Is that what you think? That deaf people can't keep their hands to themselves?'

She wouldn't say. She was flummoxed, pink with embarrassment and, strange to say, at that moment, I pitied her, a woman terrified of her own shadow, a woman who would break out in a cold sweat at the mention of divine retribution. And now, if I were to see her again, what would I say to her, assuming we were on speaking terms? I think I would urge her not to give up, to keep on searching. I would tell her that there are many paths to the one goal: peace of mind.

5

One morning I overslept and arrived late for breakfast. Hoffmann had already finished eating and had his head buried in the freshly ironed copy of *Il Messagero* that had been laid out for him as usual on the reading stand. He greeted me without looking up and, mistaking me for a chess buff, read out something about a match in Cuba. As I sat down I noticed a used coffee cup – Claudia's.

'You've missed her I'm afraid. She's out on a jaunt with Persiani – Kolya's man from the Russian embassy. You'll meet him yourself soon enough.'

Faking indifference, I asked where they had gone. Licenza – Horace's villa. They were going for a picnic and Persiani had the use of an embassy car.

'They left at the crack of dawn, I hope they didn't disturb you.'

As Hoffmann got up from the table to go to work, Alfredo brought me my boiled egg. I picked up a spoon and cracked it open; just as on the previous day it was overcooked. Claudia had given instructions to the cook on how I liked my eggs but in her absence I could not make clear what I wanted in Italian (or it could have been that Alfredo was being deliberately obtuse). He apologized and took the egg away without more ado.

I decided to give up on breakfast altogether and went to fetch the letter from Gerda that had arrived the previous day. I was brooding about Reuss. Following their chance meeting at the magic show, after which he insisted on seeing her home they had agreed to meet again for old times' sake and Reuss had somehow or other managed to wangle a complimentary seat for her at a performance of Dr Strauss' new opera at the Kroll Theatre, where Reuss was singing in the chorus. Tickets for this event were extraordinarily expensive and just as hard to come by in the normal run of things and Gerda left me in no doubt as to how much she was looking forward to the outing. Was this to punish me for staying away so long?

I was moving a wicker chair into the light, when I became aware of little Freddy, who was playing by the balcony with a toy boat.

I had mentioned him too in my letter to Zoya:

> Freddy (Friedrich) is I suppose 4 years old and also strange but in a different way, rarely speaking and never looking anyone straight in the eye, and then without any warning he will flap his hands about or stamp. I thought he might too be deaf at first, but it seems his hearing is normal although he won't come

to his mother when called and seems to prefer the maid, although even she isn't allowed to go near him when he's in one of his moods. Claudia says Philipp blames her for all this and accuses her, when they're together, of being cold towards the boy. Claudia is determined never to go through with another pregnancy after what happened, despite Hoffman's wishes for another child.

I said 'hello' but he ignored me completely and carried on with his game.

Claudia's unexpected disappearance had put my nose out of joint. What was the matter with me? Was I jealous of this Persiani? And what was Hoffmann playing at anyway putting temptation in her way. Was that why he could never look me in the eye, as though he were the guilty party? The idiosyncrasies of her love making alone would have made her vulnerable to detection. She took the precaution I noticed always to wear blouses with high collars and never risked exposing an inch of flesh above the wrist. But how, when they were alone together could she possibly conceal the welts and blotches from all the nibbling and biting?

Watching the boy out the corner of one eye, I became aware that he was holding the toy paddle steamer the wrong way up.

'The funnel should be at the top,' I explained. He stared at me and repeated what I had said word for word. Thinking he had failed to understand, I left my seat and tried to take the toy from him to demonstrate but he immediately began screaming and waving his arms about and nothing I could do would calm him until Sandra came out and dragged him, protesting all the while, indoors.

It was that evening over dessert that I brought up Kolya's visits to Italy as a child. (How we envied him missing school.)

'They stayed at the Albergo della Sibilla, he and his uncles. It's still there, albeit under new management. Kolya went to have another look at it actually, the last time he was here. Didn't he, Claudi?'

I announced my plan to borrow a bike and do a little exploring on my own. I was smarting from being left out of the excursion to Licenza and had been looking all day for a way to exact my revenge. As it happened, the day had been spoilt by archaeologists working at the site and making it next to impossible to get more than a glimpse of the precious mosaic. The picnic too had to be abandoned on account of the dust, leaving them little choice but to drive to Subiaco for lunch, by which time Claudia was exhausted.

When she left the table complaining of a headache, Hoffmann had more to say about Kolya: 'She took his death very badly, worse than Greta in some respects.'

It was the first time he had referred to Kolya's death.

'I wouldn't allow the women near him until he'd been thoroughly cleaned up. I went to the hospital alone and to be honest I didn't recognise him at first.'

Quite apart from the blows to the head, they had broken his jaw, ruptured a kidney, given him one hell of a beating.

'Bruises all over him, according to the doctors, one of the worst cases they had seen. I was surprised he survived as long as he did to be honest – I think they were, too.'

'Who found him?'

'A street sweeper, or a night watchman, I don't remember. He saw two men making off from the scene in a damned hurry. Kolya was lying there unconscious until the police arrived. Nothing was taken even his rings and his pocket watch.'

'Nothing at all? Then he wasn't robbed.'

'That may have been their intention but no.'

'If it wasn't, there's the question of motive,' I said, thinking aloud.

'It's a miracle they didn't rifle through his valuables.'

'Who do you mean, his attackers?'

'No, no the street sweeper or whoever it was. Maybe he was after a reward. Hoodlums, savages.'

I decided to raise the subject of Freitas' "calling card". 'There was nothing else on his person – a note, for instance?'

'What "note"?'

'Just a thought.'

'We were hoping you might be able to shed some light... Did he say anything in Berlin? Did he hint at anything untoward?'

'He seemed a bit distracted. But then we only met by chance. He was keen for us to meet again though after his trip to Italy.'

'In his most lucid moments, he was insistent that you should have the box. He kept coming back to it – to the box.'

I asked how the police investigation was getting on. Had anyone been arrested?

Not so far as he knew. This really wasn't good enough. I found his reticence baffling.

'But...but aren't you anxious to find out who did this?'

'Of course.'

'Well then? Who do they suspect, local villains? Opportunists?'

'We've bribed the right officials if that's what you mean. Even so, it's a waste of time. The Carabiniere will simply produce a couple of recidivists from their gaols and pin the crime on them. The embassy is conducting its own investigation – discreetly, behind the scenes.'

'You do know Kolya was involved in politics when he was living in Trieste?'

'Trieste, that was years ago. Besides, what has politics to do with it? Look, not a word about our conversation to Claudi, is that clear? I don't want her getting upset. Leave Kolya out of it altogether where she's concerned, is my advice.'

6

The hotel was perched precariously on a rocky outcrop directly overlooking the gorge and was popular with artists as well as tourists. I found it without difficulty – it was only a five minute ride from the town and was visible most of the way. After chaining the bike to the bridge, I made the final climb via a cobbled pathway, and came to a brick gateway with part of the plaster missing and a niche with a bell that could be rung late at night to alert the caretaker. After rattling the knocker I pushed the door open to see a large courtyard with outbuildings on my left, while to my right was a patio leading to a dining room with a terrace and small garden. I remember a servant girl in an apricot dress smiling shyly at me as she swept a patch of tiled floor, also a discarded wagon wheel propped up against a post, a pair of rocking chairs with wicker seats and a leather saddle hanging by a door. The postman had arrived just ahead of me and pulled out a handful of letters from his satchel. He slammed the reception bell, which disturbed the caged songbirds but failed to alert the desk clerk. It was the time of day when a hotel is at its quietest, when the rooms have been vacated and the guests have dispersed after leaving their luggage with the porter (there was no sign of him either), to go sightseeing or hunt frantically for last minute souvenirs. I passed the time admiring the mounted photographs in the hallway of jockeys, race horses, grandstands, paddocks and winner's enclosures until a tradesman appeared lugging a potted aspidistra across the floor and nodded in the direction of the bar. I thought I could make out a faint crackling sound which I took to be the telephone ringing after I collided with a self-important man in a frock coat hurrying in from the garden. It was a bit early for a drink so I drew a crisp hundred lira note from my wallet and asked for a bottle of Peroni. The barman glanced up at the clock and with a show of reluctance unlocked the cabinet. It took only a little coaxing to persuade him to join me for a drink, though he kept his glass under the counter as a precaution. The beer was warm and flat; while he was looking for the ice tongs, I asked him about the photographs. They belonged to the current owner, a Swede named Hölström. He had bought the hotel several years earlier as an investment, spending most of his time in Scandinavia where he owned a major shipping line. Carlo treated me to an entertaining account of Hölström's successes at the race track. The owner of a string of horses, one of which had won the Italian Derby, he had a stud farm in the Campagna, which Carlo, not adverse to the odd flutter himself I discovered, was very proud of.

I asked about the guests.

'We're a bit out of the way here. Most of our clients are day trippers from Rome who miss their connection. We do get the odd celebrity though. The poet d'Annunzio stayed a couple of years ago and before him, I'm told, the Russian composer Tchaikovsky.'

I finished my drink and wandered into the garden, picturing Kolya as a boy jumping over the flower beds (he was very keen on jumping) until Uncle Modya put a stop to the fun and games for his daily dose of speech training. I sat down on a green wooden bench and here he is, Uncle Modya standing before me in a navy blue bowler with a matching serge coat and tie, a cane at his side and with a copy of the Head's book, *Quelqes mots sur la Methode d'Articulation dans l'Enseignement* tucked under his arm… And behind him Mr Boil-on-the-Bum, I recalled with a smile. Because now we were at Fouviere, in the little park that slopes down to the Saone from the Basilica de Notre Dame. We were sunbathing, Kolya and I lying face down on the grass, a little way apart from the other boys in the group. I remember Kolya pulling up a stalk of grass and sucking on the end, pretending it was a cigarette, while telling a silly, but hilarious story about his Uncle Modya, then going on to do a funny imitation of the friend – "Goldtooth" – trying to sit down with a boil on his backside.

There would be an even better view of the waterfall from the balustrade, I decided. I stood up to take a look and just then, although the sky was completely clear, a rainbow appeared arcing over the gorge, a beautiful sight.

'Do you think there are still people who think that way about us, people like Lycurgus?' Kolya was frowning, his mood darker.

We had been reading about Lycurgus' decree at school, the one about defective children being abandoned at birth or tossed over a cliff. I had barely been paying attention and was surprised to find that Kolya had taken it to heart. The next time we played the theatre game in which "Goldtooth" was always the wicked uncle, Kolya inserted a new scene where they're hauling the boy to the edge of a cliff. 'Don't you dare kick or wriggle you little pipsqueak or you will dash your brains out,' were the lines that were assigned to me as I assumed the role of Uncle Modya.

This, I now realised, was where it had happened.

7

The following Monday there was a change of routine at Hoffmann's. Sandra brought breakfast to my room at around seven thirty on his instructions. I was still trying to figure out what was going on when, about half an hour later, he appeared in person and, after perching awkwardly on the end of the bed, asked me what arrangements I had made for travelling on to Rome. I was so taken aback by the abruptness of the question that I was literally lost for words. Not to worry, he explained chummily, everything had been arranged. There being no railway station at Tivoli, trains bound for Rome left from Subiaco, a couple of hours' drive away. Fortunately, there was still time to make the daily connection if I got a move on, so I should finish my breakfast *toute suite* and pack, before meeting him outside the house.

It should have been a pleasant trip as it was sunny enough and the weather warm enough to have the top down, but I was put out by the abruptness and manner of my departure, which I suspected was Claudia's doing and so was all the more alarmed when Hoffmann himself brought her up in the conversation. I felt the grip on my arm as he apologized on her behalf for not seeing me off. 'She seems to be rather under the weather today. She's developed a bit of a rash, caught the sun I expect. Anyway, she's refusing to get out of bed so you'll have to make do with her best wishes.'

He went on to explain the arrangements that had been made for me on my arrival in Rome. I was to stay in a villa which the German government had recently bought and converted to an art school with ateliers and workshops. I would be happy there, Hoffmann assured me, on account of the grounds which were 'magnificent'. Persiani would "take me in hand" during my stay in Rome.

'Organizing people is his forte,' Hoffmann reminded me cheerfully as we motored on through the countryside.

8

The Russian embassy was in a quiet side street, near the Piazza Navona but an inconvenient distance from my digs in the Villa Massimo.

Persiani was dressed in a black morning coat, striped trousers, a grey vest and matching necktie, and spats. I assumed this was standard office dress for a man in his position, although with a carnation in his buttonhole he might have been mistaken for the best man at a society wedding. After shaking hands, he showed me around. There were pillars of Sienna marble, a tapestry to do with Raphael and a portrait of one of the Tsars by a Russian artist whose name I have forgotten.

I allowed the flunky to take my coat but hung on to my hat, a Fedora, which I had bought on Zoya's advice and which I liked to keep by me – fingering the brim or smoothing down the felt on the crown reassured me and helped me to concentrate on what was being said. I had even given my new hat a name – "Alphonse".

I glanced at the underside of my wrist where I had scratched a list of prompts (the idea came from an Inspector Werder mystery, *The Golden Bullet*): Last known movements. State of mind. Police? Why in Rome?

Persiani had been a pupil at one of Russia's top schools and, according to Hoffmann, had excelled at Latin. They used to talk it at home, the entire family, every evening at dinner.

He handed me a typed document which I suppose he might have called "Kolya's itinerarium".

He had been away for about six weeks in all and covered a hell of a lot of ground – Parma, Modena, the Po valley, Mantua, Milan. Mostly it had been cattle auctions, agricultural exhibitions, rotary dinners... It was a lecture tour, Persiani explained, sponsored by the Russian Chamber of Commerce.

'Kolya's estate, Grankino, is one of the most profitable agricultural estates in the Ukraine, possibly in the whole of Russia. It's held up by the government to be a shining example of what the reforms currently underway might achieve, given a fair wind.'

More to the point, perhaps, the Minister of Agriculture was a personal acquaintance of Kolya.

Glancing at the schedule, I asked why there was an asterisk by the name Grassini. He was an American businessman with a villa near Lake Como. Back home he owned a huge chemical concern and was hoping, with Kolya's help, to secure a major foothold in the Russian fertilizer market.

At that point Persiani got up abruptly to answer the phone.

'That was Rachmaninov on the blower,' he said sweeping back into the room, as if a famous concert pianist breezing into town was the most natural thing in the world. 'He wants the piano tuner again – that'll be the third time this week.'

Rachmaninov was recuperating from a gruelling European concert tour.

'He's been here a month already so it looks as though we're lumbered. By the way, take a look at his hands if you get the chance, they say he can play a chord spanning twelve white notes.'

Persiani's hands were equally remarkable, albeit in a different way, the fingers long and slender – the way he steepled them while thinking reminded me of a painting by Durer hung on the wall of my parent's bedroom, except his were a young man's hands.

As third secretary, Persiani was in charge of making Rachmaninov's stay pleasant and comfortable, from ensuring a regular supply of his favourite brand of cigarettes to finding a tennis partner for his wife.

'Better than taking the ambassador's dog for a walk, I suppose but a bit of a far cry from high diplomacy.'

Persiani had entered the diplomatic service as a "high flier". I wouldn't have been so sniffy, to my way of thinking the Rome embassy was a plum posting.

9

The trouble I had with that bloody suitcase! The grip was facing the wrong way so I had to lie on my side and try to grab it with both hands. But it had got caught somehow on a bedpost and in the end I had to inch it free. And all the while, the sun streaming through the skylight. He should have taken better care of a suitcase of that quality – calf leather dyed olive green (the Italian colour), with thick straps and brass corners. In *Tietz* or *Kaufhaus des Westens* something of that quality would set you back 100 Marks. I brushed the dust off my hands and drank a glass of water.

But I'm getting ahead of myself. There was someone Persiani thought I would like to meet, one of my old school masters from Lyon. Freycinet was the name on the card.

When I arrived he was still teaching; but he had left instructions that I was to be shown around the *Istituto dei Sordi* by a monitor who wore a badge which proudly announced, "I can speak".

Institution – a word I loathe. Encountering it is like… like opening an innocuous-looking envelope and finding news of the death of a friend or a ransom demand from a blackmailer. This *Istituto* would have left me with a favourable impression, even if it was run by Roman Catholic priests and nuns, were it not for seeing two of the children being admonished for using sign language in the corridor. Could this really still be such a big issue?

'Brand, of course I remember you!' He said it as if he meant it, as if I had been a favourite pupil of his or one of the school's success stories, like the boy who went on to graduate in engineering and made a career in building bridges. Later I wondered whether he had me confused with someone else.

The vigorousness of his handshake surprised me as he was elderly and quite bald and I would never have recognised him at all had we not been introduced. I had a vague recollection of a much younger man with dark hair, other than that Freycinet had made little impression on me and even now I was unable to recall anything more about him, not even his nickname or what his weaknesses were.

We climbed four or five flights of stairs to the attic where he and several of the other teachers had rooms. A single sweeping glance was enough to take it all in: one iron bedstead, one wash stand with a freshly laundered towel hanging from a brass rail, one plain wooden chair with an oval back and wobbly hind leg. On the wall was an ebony crucifix and a framed painting of Jesus, his expression reproachful but compassionate, his bleeding heart exposed and seemingly on fire. All in all, digs that would have been to the taste of those Spanish monks you see in religious paintings, ecstatic wide-eyed young men with three days of stubble and a dishevelled look, dressed in hair shirts and brown sacking. Yet for all that, there was something about the lack of clutter I found appealing to the point where I even got to thinking that I too might be comfortable in these surroundings.

10

We skirted round the subject of Kolya's passing as if by pre-arranged agreement.

Out of the blue Freycinet had received a letter from him with an offer of work at the *Istituto*. Kolya had been one of the school governors, and the patron of a variety of progressive deaf causes. I was still reflecting on what he would have made of the incident in the corridor – Freycinet seemed to read my mind:

'Konradi was a realist,' he signed, following it with a shrug of resignation. 'But he hadn't given up the fight; far from it. He had the enterprising notion of using the cinema to make the case for signing, as a language in its own right.'

Kolya had been prepared to put up most of the money himself and had got as far as looking for a director in the United States.

'What will happen to that now I wonder?'

I suggested taking it up with Hoffmann.

The suitcase had been a present from Kolya. Freycinet was using it for storing memorabilia (no wonder it had been difficult to shift) – press cuttings, magazines, certificates, old exercise books... I was in for a long afternoon.

He invited me to draw my chair closer to the bed on which he perched, the first album balanced precariously in his lap.

I was astonished to see how my old school had changed beyond recognition. In my day "Chateau Perache" consisted of no more than a couple of town houses with the partition walls knocked down. Since then Tobler had relocated to open country near the village of Villaubain. These new premises, as Freycinet now showed me, were more deserving of the title *Institute*. Apart from the school buildings themselves, which were extensive, there were workshops, a prayer hall, a sawmill and a market garden where inmates judged incapable of learning a trade were set to work. Another novelty we found disturbing: the blind and the feeble–minded now rubbed shoulders with the hard of hearing (still referred to in the prospectus as 'deaf mutes' Freycinet pointed out) and there were adults as well as children, although at a world congress Tobler had steam-rollered through a resolution to strictly segregate the sexes.

Frankly, it was Tobler's international reputation as sage and prophet that had taken me aback, until Freycinet let me in on what had long been an open secret, namely Tobler's ties with the freemasons on the Lyon city council.

Were these the same local dignitaries before whom we were paraded and put through our paces to demonstrate the superiorities of 'The Method' and Tobler's other experiments? I had finally placed Freycinet. He is sitting in his form room, his pupils gathered in a semi-circle around him. We troop in from a neighbouring classroom and each of us in turn is ushered forward to place our fingers on the fret board of Monsieur's violin while he draws his bow and plays a single sustained note. And there the memory ends – I have no idea of the purpose of the experiment, only of it taking place.

'I was asking about your father – he was a sea captain, I think?'

I put him right. Time was getting on and the questions I still had for him were burning a hole in my wrist. I wanted him to talk about Kolya's mother. I didn't remember him getting many letters from home and, when he did, they seemed to upset him.

But Freycinet wasn't much help as he had no recollection of ever meeting her.

A strange thing, how whenever we acted out his favourite *Tsar Saltan* from *Illustrated Russian Fairy Tales* I had the feeling we were involved in another story, an episode from his own life. Why was that? Each performance began the same way with a picnic in the woods, Kolya insisted on it. The prince had dismissed his courtiers for the day and was taking his mother on a picnic. First they had to pick mushrooms. Grankino perhaps?

'There was something though – it had to do with passports and

Russian wives needing the permission of their husbands to travel. She was no longer around even though it had been her idea to send Kolya to Tobler in the first place.'

I asked him what he meant by "not around".

'Now I remember. She had moved to the Cote d'Azur to set up house with another man. There was a divorce, very messy and acrimonious and Kolya was taken out of school for a while by his tutor.'

This would account for the stay in Italy.

'Then the father died and something extraordinary happened, Tchaikovsky was appointed guardian.'

Tchaikovsky? He had lost me.

'Not the musician, his younger brother. He used to visit us from time to time, the composer I mean, he wasn't famous in those days. He would spoil Konradi rotten with presents and such like – expensive toys, but also practical items: an eiderdown, pillowslips, always of the highest quality.'

He was losing me again. 'You mentioned a tutor and a guardian. Then, how does Tchaikovsky fit in?'

'I mean Modest Tchaikovsky – you don't forget a name like that.'

I thought immediately of the waterfall and "Uncle Modya", but Freycinet was again off on another track.

'If you must follow Tobler's Method, you have to put your back into it. That Tchaikovsky was one for the short cut. We always suspected as much but it wasn't until we tested Konradi on diphthongs that we caught him out. There's an entire chapter devoted to it in Tobler's book, with exercises. Tchaikovsky had simply left it out. If you ask me Konradi spent far too much time out of school travelling. It wasn't good for the boy, he was a great nuisance to us when he got back from those trips. Couldn't settle to anything.'

11

'All this once belonged to Prince Dolgoruky,' said Persiani waving vaguely in the direction of the building behind him. We were strolling in the embassy gardens at the time. 'The story goes that he forfeited it after losing to the emperor at cards – probably apocryphal but, as the Italians say, *si non e vero, e ben trovato.*'

There was a good deal more history to the place and not a few colourful owners, among them a dotty dowager countess with a saintly reputation who, whenever she went out, was followed through the streets by urchins, vagabonds and beggar women.

I was all too aware that, in entertaining me in this way, Persiani was being courteous beyond the call of duty. Not to put too fine a point on it, I was making a bit of a nuisance of myself. But after meeting Freycinet, I had the feeling I might finally be on to something, without knowing exactly what.

We returned indoors and I asked Persiani how he was coping with Rachmaninov's visit.

'Things have been a lot easier since he moved into Modest Ilych's apartment on the Pincio. Sergey Vasilievich can hardly contain himself. "The flat is just as it was," he told me, "with the original furnishings intact, including his brother's piano and writing desk. Wonderful views too...." '

Modest again. I knew it! 'Would that be Kolya's uncle?'

'Well, yes, except that he's not his real uncle. Modest Ilych has known Sergey Vasilievich since his time at the Moscow conservatory. They even collaborated on an opera, *Francesca da Rimini*. Modest Ilych wrote the libretto.'

Another coincidence. I told Persiani what I remembered of the Dante film.

'That episode is a Russian favourite. We can all quote the lines *"Nessun maggior dolore che ricordarsi del tempo felice nella miseria.* No greater sorrow than to remember a time of happiness in misery". Sorrow is meat and drink to Sergey Vasilievich – we call him the Undertaker.'

Tchaikovsky... Rachmaninov... what a lot of musical gossip I had for Gerda. Trump that Reuss! I never did get her Rachmaninov's autograph. She had sent me to Italy with a shopping list: Puccini, Mascagni, Leoncavallo – if he was still alive – in that order of precedence. At the time I wasn't sure whether Modest Ilych would cut it with Gerda seeing he wasn't a composer, so I had set my sights instead on Rachmaninov, to counter Reuss who was pursuing Busoni in Berlin, one pianist- composer for another...

12

'It must have fallen down the back of the chair,' I suggest – lamely, as that is precisely where Gerda found the flyer.

Rome. The Caffè Greco. Memories, long suppressed but always threatening to surface, like rubber balls held under in a swimming pool. First up, the black poodle with the diamond collar, nigger hair and eyes as expressionless as currants... *Frou Frou.* Then Molly, a petit-four on a plate balanced precariously on knobbly knees, her smile a cross between a simper and a grimace, lady-like in her attentions, tell tale wrinkles under made-up eyes.

Gerda is doing a bit of cleaning and tidying for me as she does from time to time, even though we now share the same home. Habit, I suppose. She wipes her brow with the back of one hand, leaving a few stray hairs sticking to her forehead. She is about to hand the flyer over, but holds back. I should not have snatched. Now I have given the game away. It was me who shoved the flyer under the cushion in the first place when Trautmann had called unexpectedly. What embarrasses me even now, although I should know better, is the line drawing of a waiter holding a tray aloft, at shoulder height – wasp waist, hair parting on the girl's side, hand on hip. Even a blockhead like Trautmann would pick up on that. 'The more you look at it,' I hear him saying in that nasally voice of his, 'the more you see it, the more the fella looks as if he is about to do a twirl.' Gerda tugs a handkerchief from the front her pocket of her apron, wipes off a thick coating of dust, considers. 'If only Reuss had his figure,' is her only comment before getting on with the cleaning. I am off the hook.

13

'Signore Tchaikovsky? The party at table 17 – *como siempre.*'

It was the waiter in the line drawing, I swear, who ushered me towards the velvet curtain which divided the front and back rooms of the Greco. The front room was a public bar where the plain wooden counter, with none of your modern brass fittings, was as homely as aunty's sideboard. Goethe himself would have recognised it. He was a regular back then as he had lodgings at the far end of the street. (It's all in the booklet I picked up on the Piazza Navona.) It tickled me, Theo Brand, to imagine the author of *Young Werther* in his shepherd's hat and buckle shoes peering up at the smoky ceiling painting or discoursing (Goethe always 'discourses') on truth, beauty and the rest of it. But when I passed from here into the adjoining room, it was like the curtain going up in the theatre to reveal the stage for the first time: marble floors, chandeliers, armchairs and settles upholstered in red velvet, paintings and china vases, not unlike the pieces I had been shown by Persiani at the Russian Embassy.

There was no need to count to seventeen, each table, had its own three-pronged candelabra and attached to the central prong was a number. Passing from one compartment to the next I was reminded of the restaurant car of a train; here too the customers read while they ate, made small talk, dozed. Table seventeen was occupied but no one bore even a passing resemblance to the moustachioed gent in the blue suit and matching bowler hat who used to pick Kolya up from school.

It was spur of the moment to exaggerate my disability tin front of the waiter, cocking my head to one side while raising my voice a notch or two above the level strictly necessary in the hubbub of competing voices. Of course in an Inspector Werder mystery Modest Ilych's chums would have been 'revealing all', but picking up on secret conversations only happens to deaf people in films, like the one about the valet who saves the day by lip-reading a kidnap plot. Actually the two intense Bohemians I was observing were holding forth about a statue of David in Florence. The highbrow stuff itself has never fazed me – it was common currency in the Romanisches Haus where the Theosophical Society held meetings. It was more that what the 'Davids' had to say was of no interest. I focused instead on the straight-backed soldierly fellow the waiters referred to as *Il Barone* and addressed as *Eccelenza.* Head erect, hands planted firmly on his knees, his spit and polish cheeks and waxed moustache reminded me of a wooden doll in a toy box. Oblivious to the 'Davids' he was calmly enjoying a cigar while gazing benignly across at Molly, like a doting husband still fond of his wife after many years of marriage. Molly meanwhile, from what I could see of her, was squinting at the message on a postcard.

What I had overlooked was that I too was being observed – in a mirror, by a fourth person at the table with his back to me.

It was this *Kerl* who now spun round to eyeball me with a stare like the bulldog on the front cover of *Simplicissimus*, flashing fury, indignation and pain in the same instant, as if I had stepped on a paw. I dived for cover behind Baedeker – too late, he was padding over to my table and before I knew it, a hand had locked onto my arm like a jaw snapping shut and I was being propelled towards his associates.

A brusque interrogation followed.

'Watch this one.' He left me standing in front of them like an abject schoolboy caught carving an obscenity on a desk. Then he was on his way with the "Davids" as acolytes.

He was on the point of leaving, a protective arm extended around one of the boys, when he snarled, 'Do you hear? Don't say I didn't warn you.'

Did I imagine it, or was there the glint of a gold tooth?

14

I was waiting for Persiani as arranged at the Spanish steps. When he arrived, I was fending off a beggar and needed rescuing. (Baedecker warning: Beware pickpockets especially in the vicinity of the Piazza di Spagna).

'We had to stand for the best part of an hour,' said Persiani by way of apology. 'Babington's is a rendez-vous for Thomas Cook tours.' He had been with his English counterpart for their weekly get-together in the Tea Rooms.

He suggested we climb the Pincio for the view. But at the foot of the steps Persiani gave me a nudge. A tall man in a black Homburg was coming out of a neighbouring house in the company of his two daughters and their mother.

'Rachmaninov. Now you can see why we call him "The Undertaker". I won't introduce you, if you don't mind. I still need to find his wife a tennis partner.'

'I'd have thought composing at the same desk as Tchaikovsky would be a bit intimidating.'

'Pyotr Ilych rated him highly at the conservatory.'

We watched them get into a cab, then resumed our stroll.

It was a relief frankly to be leaving the neighbourhood of the Caffè

Greco. But I wasn't to escape so easily. Persiani wanted to know what I had done there to offend Prince Chersky. I pretended not to know who he was talking about but of course I had made the connection: 'Simplicissimus' = Chersky. He had complained about me to the ambassador, mistaking me for a journalist. I was completely at a loss.

'Not to worry it won't go any further. Only be careful in your dealings with Modest Ilych. You've seen his friends. If only they weren't so outré. It gets them into all kinds of trouble.

That's why Chersky is on his guard.'

He wen on to tell me an anecdote about an encounter between Modest Ilych and a footman. Some details escape me but it ended in an assault charge which had to be hushed up.

'Luckily the servant wasn't carrying a knife, they kill for less – Calabrians, not footmen.'

15

No sooner had "Simplicissimus" left the Caffè Greco than the atmosphere changed instantly. With exaggerated courtesy, the Baron rose to his feet, gave me a long appraising look, then shook me firmly by the hand. More than firmly, his handshake was crushing and belied his rather gentle, almost sentimental demeanour. This was enough too to reassure Molly who had been adding a few touches to her makeup with the aid of a compact mirror. Now she too seized my hand, then pulled me down beside her and patted me consolingly on the knee, as if I had been thrown over.

'Modestina has taken off without a word of explanation.' She handed me the postcard. It had been franked in Sorrento and was addressed to Miss Molly, care of Caffè Greco.

As I handed it back, Molly raised her eyes to heaven, then fluttered her lashes and formed her carmine lips into a stagey pout.

'Isn't it beastly of him, leaving a girl in the lurch like that and without a penny to live on?'

I studied her more closely. There was something peculiar about her smile – a cross between a simper and a grimace, and while the feint down on her upper lip was not uncommon in women from

Southern Europe, her laugh was accompanied by wildly exaggerated facial distortions. But it was only when I caught sight of the little wisps of hair on her wrists that my suspicions were confirmed: Molly was a man, a female impersonator like a turn I had seen at the Variety – the "Venus de Milo".

16

We had left the Belvedere and had gone on to admire the classical statues in the Borghese gardens. Fortunately there was tree shade as it was getting hot. The air though was fragrant, deliciously so. I wished I had learned the names of flowers – I could have written to Zoya about them. We stopped only once for Persiani to point out a favourite fountain of his in the garden of Venus. From where I was standing, I could already make out a monument at the far end of a grassy path which struck me as familiar, but it was only when we got closer that I recognised it. It was the obelisk on the postcard that Kolya had received from the woman whose name began with a "P".

We sat down on a bench nearby while Persiani told me the story of how the column came to be in Rome.

'Antinous was a youth of extraordinary beauty who caught the Emperor's eye while still a boy. The hieroglyphs probably allude to his death in Egypt in tragic circumstances. One school of thought suggests suicide, possibly at the Emperor's bidding. But there's no hard evidence.'

'But if he was the Emperor's favourite...'

'...Why would he order him to kill himself? These are just traditions. What's extraordinary is what happened after his death.

Hadrian pronounced him a god and a religious cult grew up at the site where his death had occurred until eventually an entire city was named after him.'

Persiani's knowledge of the classical world never failed to amaze me and he took infinite pains to make sure I was following.

'The cult continued to flourish. Throughout the ancient world, games and competitions were held in his honour, medallions and coins were struck, and people worshipped at shrines and temples dedicated to his memory.'

'What happened to the city?'

'Like Rome itself, it eventually fell into ruins and was plundered for its stone and marble. There are few traces of it nowadays, I'm sorry to say. The French delivered the coup de grace during the Napoleonic Wars.'

17

It took a good half hour to get from the gardens to the embassy. To be honest I was feeling a little out of condition and had to resort to fanning myself from time to time with "Alphonse". Along the way we talked about bicycles. Persiani was right. It had been close to madness on my part to consider cycling in Rome with its cobbled streets, reckless drivers and hilly terrain. He was interested to know how I managed in traffic with my disability and I explained about fixing a small mirror to the handlebars to compensate.

At Villa Dolgoruky we were served tea in the Russian manner from a boiling samovar.

I had asked to see the police report on Kolya's death and Persiani duly handed it over, a disappointingly meagre sheaf of papers bound by a black ribbon. I thumbed through the foolscap pages, neatly typed but to my frustration, not translated. As I had the feeling Persiani was on the point of sharing a confidence, I thought it better not to mention this. Sure enough, he beckoned me to accompany him beyond the confines of the reception area into an office with a map of Russia that took up an entire wall. Persiani intimated that what we were after was under lock and key and for our eyes only.

Greek Notions of Love was by an Englishman. Modest Ilych had left it behind in the apartment and, fearing that Rachmaninov would come across it in the course of his stay, had begged Persiani to go in person to retrieve the "limited edition". The text was illustrated with photographs of life models posing in the manner of Classical sculptures. All the models were male.

My first reaction was that, as dirty books go, it was a pretty tame one. The private parts were fuzzy, the poses not so different from those of strongmen on the covers of sporting magazines. Then, tracing a line of text with a finger, Persiani translated for my benefit, "the chest, developed by gymnastic exercises, is broad and swelling, the breasts project beyond the shoulders in a massive arch."

It was all a bit of a joke to him, but recalling my own "art photographs" which were far more compromising, with nothing left to the imagination, not the bush, nor even the pimple on the backside, my heart beat faster and I am sure I was blushing.

18

REUSS. I scratched the name with the nib of the dip pen. Then another attack, this time with under-scorings forceful enough to tear the paper. "Reuss" to me, but no longer to Gerda; since the outing to the Kroll Opera House, it was "Heinrich" and before long it would be "Heini". Yes, things had gone from bad to worse. Something else I'd noticed. There were no more doodles in the margins – no more hooked noses and Jew lips. And "Guess what..." she went on breathily, "Heinrich had a small solo role in *Ariadne auf Naxos*. His name even appeared in the programme: A wigmaker – Herr Reuss!"

I asked myself if Gerda wasn't courting Reuss to punish me, or exaggerating her feelings, piling on the endearments for effect. If only I could be sure. But without returning home to assess the situation, how was I to find out what was going on between them? And I couldn't go home before I had acquitted myself of an obligation. I needed a theory that would explain the box and Kolya's death at the same time. Otherwise how was I to justify myself to Hoffman and the family?

I kept returning to the same question: What was it Kolya had been on the point of telling me in Berlin – a confidence that might have saved his life? Was this the matter weighing on his mind at around 11pm on the night of the embassy reception, when he left complaining of feeling unwell? Was "feeling unwell" an excuse? Or was he meeting someone? Or was it simply that Modest Ilych had spoilt the evening for him. 'We could hardly invite one and not the other,' Persiani had said. 'Keeping them apart at dinner was no problem as I personally saw to the seating arrangements, but when Rachmaninov was invited to play, it was a bit of a free-for-all, frankly.' 'Keeping them apart?' I had asked. They had not spoken for years apparently. There had been a major falling out over money.

19

Do you remember setting the mug down on the rough surface, your legs almost giving way from under you as you went out into the courtyard, conscious that the boy was watching you from behind the counter? You worked the pump, shoving your head under the tap and submitting to the freezing water as it coursed through your hair and down your back, until your shirt too was wringing wet. You rinsed out your mouth and, despite a raging thirst, spat.

When I returned from the yard, both the boy and his mother were standing motionless in the centre of the room, hands clasped, heads bowed. It was only as they knelt down that I understood that the Angelus bell must have sounded. I waited for them to finish the prayer, then, addressing both of them at the same time, asked for *acqua, molto acqua*. It took a devil of a long time in coming and when it did I drank long and hard, straight from the earthenware jug.

Maybe Gerda had been right about the call of home. She had warned me that there would come a time when I would miss my friends. She meant friends I could rely on, friends for life. She meant Rudi and the cycling club crowd who had set a place in my honour at the annual dinner and toasted my absence with a special rendition of *'The crazy cyclist'*.

20

It was a two-hour walk from the embassy to the crime scene at Trastevere. I got there with the help of a sketch pinned to the back of the police report. When I arrived, there was nothing to see by but a sliver of moon when the clouds shifted and the gas lamps burning on the bridge. There was building work going on all along the embankment and I had to scramble over mounds of earth to reach the water's edge. I could make out the silhouette of ... a hoist it may have been, or pile driver and thought I heard a dog barking behind a wooden fence. As I rubbed rock-slime and gravel from the palms of my hands, a thought occurred. Were his clothes, his evening clothes, impregnated with the river smell – sulphur, mud, mulch?

He had put up a fight, his injuries attested to that. They must have had a taste for blood. The street-sweeper who found him had mistaken his prone form for a tree trunk until he heard a groan. A tree trunk in a stony wasteland.

I had the feeling I was being watched. I looked back towards the bridge and saw a woman leaning casually on the parapet like a visitor contemplating the view. I feigned disinterest and, with the walking stick I had taken along for my own protection, idly prodded the ground in front of me. Waiting. The blood-rush, the old itch, the hard-on. I kept my back to her until I could taste her cheap scent.

'Cuanto?' It came out dry-mouthed and thick – probably she took me for a drunk. Losing patience, she made a grab for my wrist. I let her, went along. Big mistake. We were caught in a beam of light; or rather I was caught, the whore had made a bolt for it.

The torch was beckoning from the riverbank to the bridge and back with a persistence that could only mean the law.

Resigned I climbed back up the bank and presented myself to the waiting police officers. One lost interest and walked away, the other made a kind of salute before questioning me.

I was trying to explain why I was not carrying identification when Barkov arrived and presented what I took to be a calling card. While the policeman was examining it with the aid of his torch, Barkov was already reaching for his pocket book. With the finesse of a conjurer, he transferred a number of bank notes into the officer's hand and we were on our way.

Was it because it had been a long time since I'd heard German spoken that I had agreed to go with him? After all, it might have been a set up – the prostitute on the bridge, squaring it with the cop. What if I had refused to get into the carriage? Were Barkov's associates waiting in the shadows, ready to bundle me in if I made trouble?

21

When we got in Barkov was all apologies: he'd been meaning to… He was in the middle of … He'd not got around to…

He used his flashlight to locate the oil lamp. What he'd been meaning to do was decorate, at least that was what I assumed because the room was quite bare, except for a couple of ribbed-back chairs, a packing crate which did service as a table, a mattress which smelt faintly of urine and a wall telephone.

While he fixed us drinks (a Balkan tipple I noticed from the label on the bottle), he whistled a tune that might have been an aria, the white scarf suggesting a night at the opera.

'Are you a patriot, Brand?' I must have been slow to react because he found a piece of chalk and wrote the question out again across the wall. 'King and Fatherland? Konradi was, Russian to the core.'

It touched a nerve, patriot. There was this character, Braun, used to stand us drinks before shaking the Navy League collecting tin in front of our noses. You would see him pinning on the little blue badges with the gold anchors while mock saluting my friends as they "paid their dues". One time, not wanting to be left out, I too held out my coppers. He accepted my contribution with a certain distaste. 'You'll do your best,' is what I think he said. But my best wasn't enough to earn me my lapel pin.

We discovered we had Kolya in common.

'Extraordinary' was his response after I touched on our chance meeting in the Lustgarten. 'Why it must have been all of thirty years and you still recognized him.'

He supposed it was the ears – like the handles on those tin trophies they give out at school sports.

A joke in pretty poor taste when you come to think of it, but at the time I let it pass.

He and Kolya too went way back – Batumi, to be precise (BA-TU-MI he spelled it out on the wall). They had met on the voyage out, 'quite by chance, you understand.'

I pictured it like a scene out of *Atlantis*. They got talking and it turned out they had adjoining cabins. They agreed to a smoke on the promenade deck before dinner and by the time they docked in Constantinople they were the best of pals. He meant that he had taken Kolya under his wing.

'I'm like a jealous lover in that respect', he said, hand on heart to make sure I got the point.

He topped up my glass – of Slivovitz, if that's the one that tastes of almonds. I was succumbing to a delicious numbness. The tension in my back and shoulders had disappeared, my feet were tingling pleasantly, even my breathing had returned to normal. Yet curiously my brain was working overtime and I found that I was talking about everything and nothing in particular, talking for the sake of it. Out it all poured about Zoya, the buffed-up version where she owned the dressmaker's shop catering exclusively for the rich and famous, had her own apartment on the Piazza del Duomo, didn't wear a corset and behaved provocatively in public.

Barkov lit up a cigarette. I picked up the discarded yellow packet to find that it was actually a wooden box, covered with a layer of glazed paper and bearing the trademark *Kyriazi Frères, Alexandria.* Another coincidence. Lindstrom had been on the look out for that very brand in Trieste.

What had I been doing in Trieste? Barkov asked.

I explained about the photograph, how I had tracked down the studio on Piazza Ponterrosso that led me first to Freitas, then to Zoya. My account flowed as naturally as the unrolling of a carpet and I was far from done.

I drained my Slivovitz before moving on to the strike, how it started in the shipyards and ended up becoming general. 'The last thing the Austrians wanted was a work stoppage on one of their warships. But sending in the army though...'

'An admirable précis. But where is Konradi in all this? Apart from getting caught up in the excitement.'

Helping them out financially, according to Zoya.

'There, you see. Why would anyone in his right mind want to bankroll... I mean, he's on the other side isn't he, Konradi? He's a landowner *and* a capitalist. He plays the stock market, or has someone do it for him. He invests. The little vineyard in Georgia, his pride and joy?'

'You mean why would he want to shell out on...?'

'The talking shop in San Giacomo. I do recall him buying a typewriter for Red Ana. An act of charity, he said, to even up the sides.'

'He was testing out a theory – about crowd psychology.'

'He was now you come to mention it. How did he put it to me about the strike? He felt the way a gardener might, tending plants in a hothouse while outside it's blowing a gale.'

Detached? I suggested.

'Not entirely. There's Zoya. It was an instructive experience for all concerned. I happened to be on the Corso the day after the rioting and who should I see sweeping broken glass from the front of the wedding gown shop?'

Zoya had told me she had been teaching needlework in an orphanage.

'Versatile lady. Any other names from that time – other than the ones you've mentioned from the photo?'

I thought hard. All I could come up with was the Austrian ensign Kolya used to hang around with at the Berlitz School.

Was there a flicker of recognition before he said, 'Well if a chap can't be allowed to choose his friends...'

It no longer mattered to me. I was already on my way to formulating a theory and felt as exhilarated as when I rebuilt my uncle's bicycle, after he had dismantled it to show me how it worked. Supposing Kolya had been working for the other side. What if his murder was a reprisal? My starting point was Freycinet's recollection about Kolya taking up a long-standing invitation to visit the estate of an Italian marquis. This marquis had fallen out with his own villagers after refusing to fund a school on the grounds that it would be staffed with socialists and atheists. They held a march during Kolya's stay and a barn was set on fire.

Barkov didn't know about any *marchese*.

'But you do see the connection... with the ruckus in Milan... "Down with the capitalist bloodsucker" '

He was shaking his head. 'You think *they* bumped him off? Anarchists, black flag merchants – those hoodlums?'

Comrade Ana's lot then – Freitas?

No calling card. For Barkov that was the clincher. The clincher because to the revolutionary mind every action is a statement of intent. It seeks, rather it demands, publicity. Make it into the newspapers and you reach the street, the masses.

All the same it was murder whichever way you look at it. Someone had to be held to account.

'Do you think the Russian government takes the murder of one of its citizens lightly?'

I was almost expecting him to chalk it up, this statement delivered in the same tone, as aggressive, and pompous as his "patriot" outburst earlier in the evening.

'That's where we come in. It's our business, it's what we do.'

These words had a peculiar effect on me. They seemed to produce a physical sensation, like bringing a chill into the room. The reek of urine had become intolerable. In addition to the mattress, I noticed something else. A patch of floor had been covered with folded squares of newspaper as if to soak up a spillage or hide a stain.

'Your Russian has his own code, his own way of doing things.' Who said that? Lindstrom's friend, the one who worked for the Swedish telephone people, Ericsson. They do a lot of business in Russia. One of their top people had been ambushed in St Petersburg on his way to a meeting. His driver was shot dead. There was a ransom demand in the tens of thousands. Ericsson wanted to negotiate but the Russians wouldn't hear of it. They didn't bother with manhunts and searches, they made it known that they were holding a particular individual, a criminal boss who had links with the revolutionary underground. They lifted two of his relatives off the street, his brother and his four year old son. Then they sent a message: the brother's right thumb and a reminder that the clock was ticking...

Barkov was still talking: something about handling it ourselves, keeping it discreet for the widow's sake. 'Think what the press would make of it, a Russian magnate left for dead in "night town".'

Just what was I expecting to find there anyway? Boot prints, billy clubs floating on the Tiber?

'Poor fellow he was in a terrible state at the end. And then there was the morphine they were giving him for the pain, huge doses of the stuff. So we can't really be sure of anything can we?'

I saw where he was going with this, while Hofmann could be

relied on when it came to authenticating a Veronese...

I was breaking out in a sweat and my head was swimming. There were no windows in the room. I thought about making a run for it, but suspected him of locking the door.

Why was I here with him, alone in this room above a boarded-up wine shop, with a low-pitched roof, a reinforced door and an illegible shop sign? I recalled running my fingers over the surface of a rough brick wall while Barkov fiddled with the lock.

I must have been close to passing out because the next thing I remember is him shaking me. I thought I heard Gerda's voice, telling me I was wanted at the shop. Home...home...

Outside it was becoming light and the slaughterhouse men were arriving for work.

GRANKINO

1

At Grankino I had watched Kolya's farm workers take delivery of the American tractor, the model earmarked in the catalogue he had left behind in Tivoli.

Now the entire village gathered on the 'patch' where the local fairs were held, to see the Mogul put through its paces. "It was a source of mystery to all" reported the local newspaper, "that the tractor has no smokestack, being powered by a petrol and not a steam engine." There was a photograph alongside the article but the grainy black and white image did not do justice to the scene which was pure Repin: the cotton-wool clouds, the cornflowers shimmering in the breeze, the bellowing behemoth wreathed for the occasion in a blue silk sash, the old men gape-mouthed in wonder and the band with their motley trombones, horns, fiddles and clarinets. A Repin, except for the mangy dog that trotted up to the back paddle wheel and raised its hind leg moments before the priest arrived to give his blessing and sprinkle the chassis with holy water.

My job was to drop the documents off at the Odessa Customs House and wait for clearance before travelling on to Grankino. To expedite matters I had instructions to hand over a bulky brown envelope to an officer who would be looking out for me. There was nothing in Hoffman's instructions about arranging delivery but I was so pleased with my new role as Kolya's stand-in (and emboldened by my success with the customs), that I gave the freight company the go-head. I wasn't to know that Mondays were considered unlucky in those parts.

'Monday you son-of-a-bitch; *Ponedel'nik, ponedel'nik* – the tractor comes on Monday. Mark it on the calendar.' De Kuyper boxed the bailiff's ears for challenging my authority. But instead of *Schadenfreude* at the tongue-lashing which followed, I felt an urge to intervene on his behalf – a misunderstanding, forget it. What disconcerted me was the way he abased himself: standing cap in hand, eyes rooted to the floor, scratching his head like the obliging village idiot putting on a show to amuse his betters.

After dealing with the bailiff, the estate manager invited me to his office for tea.

The stove in the log cabin was lit because de Kuyper, a burly individual with a grey streak in his hair that reminded me of a badger, "felt the cold" although outside it was a warm spring day. Sealed in the stifling air was a smell of kerosene mixed with dog shit – or it may have been caked mud carried in on serial pairs of boots. Before I could sit down on the bench, I had to help him clear away his colleague's winter clothes. This colleague, the agronomist he explained, was up country demonstrating farm equipment and would be away for weeks.

In time I would come to see the estate office as de Kuyper's dispensary. There was a steady procession of callers, to make way for whom I was always having to give up my place on the bench. Each "consultation" was restricted to five minutes (de Kuyper kept time with an alarm clock). Most of his customers wanted nails or building materials requiring a chit which he dispensed irascibly and with reluctance while he sat bottled up in an astrakhan coat like a nasty tasting, purple-black medicine.

2

Grankino had been Hoffmann's idea. I was toying with my breakfast, wondering whether I would be able to hold any of it down, when I was handed the telegram:

RETURN IMMEDIATELY STOP. BRING EVERYTHING STOP. DEVELOPMENTS STOP. HOFFMANN

Nothing unsettles more than a telegram and Hoffmann's cablese didn't help. Did 'immediately' mean right now, or in the morning? And 'return' where – Tivoli? Berlin? As for 'developments'…

Laying my clothes out on the bed – the made-to-measure suits, waistcoats (3), silk ties and socks, the patent leather boots, I felt like a creditor with a dunning letter.

It had started with small things – over-generous tips to pretty waitresses, ordering from the à la carte menu at dinner, the trip to Rovigno where I discovered the delights of the Austrian Riviera, leaving my wallet behind in a Trieste cat house. Then I came across the Brownie box camera that I had bought in Milan, hoping to persuade Zoya to model for me like Lindstrom's girlfriend. I still hadn't worked out how to use it. I found bundles of receipts, mostly dating from the first couple of weeks, nothing at all for the camera.

Worse, I had still to come up with an explanation for Kolya's death that would pass muster with Hoffmann and justify the family's... investment.

I gave flight serious consideration but it was too late to make a final withdrawal from the Hoffmann account. If I could get to Milan under my own steam, Zoya might help me out... shopping on Via Manzoni had been her idea... Cable Gerda? Even Reuss entered my calculations.

Just then a motorcycle messenger arrived to tell me that an embassy car would shortly be taking me to Tivoli. I was to hand over my passport. When I asked why he shrugged. Those were his instructions. I panicked. Would I get it back or was it being confiscated? Was I being held? Was this Barkov's doing?

On my fourth attempt at cramming everything into the Moroccan leather suitcase ('bring everything' the telegram had said), I emptied the entire contents onto the floor in a fit of rage. I was thinking of getting the porter to lend me a hand when I noticed one of the art students at the open door trying to get my attention. He was holding out an invitation to a 'showing' of his work — canapés and champagne supper to follow. I had been hoping for a bit of company during my stay at the hostel, for one of them at least to show some curiosity about me. I suppose he was not to blame for picking the wrong moment.

3

In Hoffmann's study, or *Scriptorium* as it said in Gothic letters on the oak door, I was trying to justify myself to the back of his head. He was down on one knee, twiddling with the dials of a safe, so was unable to see the press cutting I was flourishing:

Espionage Ring Latest. Dateline Trieste.

The article, dating from a month or so back, cited the arrest of a Serbian orthodox priest in connection with the stolen plans of an Austrian warship as evidence of a spy network operating in the city against Imperial interests.

What if... so my latest theory went... What if Kolya had been recruited to spy for Russia back in his student days (I left Barkov out of it) and was murdered when he tried extricating himself from the service? It would explain the medal and the ensign.

I might have saved my breath – Hoffmann had moved away from the safe and was stacking papers before dropping them into large manila envelopes. Official-looking papers, typed and signed, some of them sealed with red wax. Each envelope had been pre-labelled: "For the port authority" "For the notary in Nikolaev" "For the estate office at Grankino" ... "For Theo Brand. Item: one passport and visa validated for travel throughout the Russian Empire, subject to the usual restrictions."

I gripped the edge of the desk to steady myself. It was as if the furnishings of the Cranach room, the carved chair, the lectern, the candlestick, the hourglass had joined in a jerky *danse macabre* that was getting between me and what Hoffmann was trying to say.

He showed me hotel reservations, train tickets, banknotes wrapped in oilskin and tied with elastic bands – Austrian currency, Hoffmann explained, and enough Russian roubles to tide me over.

He had thought of everything, even a banker's draft to be drawn on by an authorized person in Berlin to indemnify the shop against possible losses in my absence.

Hoffmann wasn't through with the surprises. He had books for me – a thick black tome and the Blue Book as I came to call it; Kolya's "diary", a cash or accounts book with ruled pink lines and feint blue squares, pocket size, the kind they sell in stationers. It had swollen from being stuffed with pasted-in advertisements, business cards, a chess puzzle and some unused Italian postage stamps. Most of the entries were written in hieroglyphs. It was only later when I was challenged at customs and had to explain what it was doing in my baggage, did it occur to me that the hieroglyphs depicted deaf signs.

Hoffmann was willing to crowbar me into it with talk of honour: didn't I owe it to my dead friend to finish what I'd started?

It was at that point I completely lost the drift. Visibly vexed, he grabbed a sheet of paper and wrote MODEST TCHAIKOVSKY in over-large block letters.

Did he take me for an idiot? I held back the urge to punch him in the face.

'Kolya's guardian...?' He was miming encouragement like a competitor in a parlour game.

'Famous brother,' I suggested, throwing in for good measure, 'composer?'

Irritated shake of the head.

I thought for a moment. 'Caffè Greco,' was all I could come up with.

Bull's-eye!

'Journalist...' he prompted.

Goldtooth had mistaken me for a journalist, so Persiani had told me, but I couldn't see what journalists had to do with Kolya.

Hoffmann explained that was why I had to go to Russia. Kolya's name had come up in connection with a scandal that originated in Russia. We were getting somewhere. A newspaperman had been asking questions. That was enough, in Hoffmann's view at least, to suggest trouble for Kolya's reputation and for his family.

One thing he was at great pains to impress upon me: I was to keep Kolya and his family out of it, *at whatever the cost!*

He was helping me balance the books, envelopes and packages, when he added, 'Remember in St Petersburg not to drink the tap water.'

4

Seven snaps is all I have. Light got in – too much exposure, the chemist reckoned. A shame that none of the film from Grankino came out because by then I had done with taking views and, ignoring Reuss's advice, was experimenting with psychic photography. I had hopes of capturing Kolya's disembodied spirit on film. What I'm left with is a pretty random assortment: the steps at Odessa; the Yevropeyskaya Hotel, waiters in the Bavarian restaurant; Poltava (the high street?); cattle drivers, there was a big fair on; a church – nothing special, just that onion domes were still a novelty; my driver and erstwhile drinking companion, Yuriy Kirillovich; and this must be the border crossing at Podvolochisk, the first station signs in Cyrillic as well as Galician. I should have taken the Jews from the Shtetl, running alongside the train with boiled eggs and roasted chickens.

There is nothing from Zoya for that time, unless you count the cutting about the spy ring that arrived without a note, and the thoughtless postcard:

How are you? Everything in Brera much the same, Tiriocchi's also.

Madame is keeping us busy. Bought a splendid fruit bowl from Leopardi.

Oh, went again to the Eden for a show – 'tip top'. Edda came, also people you don't know. Very rowdy. Everyone smoking, you wouldn't have liked it AT ALL.

Affectionately

Z.

"Seize the day", which of us had said that? And what if I had? What if I had sold up in Berlin and opened a business in Brera: "Practical yet alluring clothing for female cyclists – accelerates your good points while concealing the rest"?

So why hadn't I? Was it her I didn't trust, or myself?

I put away the photographs when one of the gardeners, Herr Stolz, stopped for a brief chat and to report on how plot 543 (Frieda's grave) was 'doing'. 'Gave the grass border a bit of a trim today, Herr Brand, now everything's spick and span.' (I'll slip him a few pfennigs at the end of the week).

Lunch as usual in Holy Trinity cemetery – a Bismarck herring sandwich, 'carry out' from the pub, no stinting on the onion and peppercorn.

When thinking of Frieda I always go back to our first meeting – it's easier to remember the other things that way. It was a bitterly cold November day, cold enough to be wearing an old woollen dressing gown over my leather apron, a pair of woollen mittens to give my aching fingers a fighting chance and – a present from my mother – an *ushanka* fur hat. Business 'front of house' had been slow that day and I had left the shop unattended so I could get on with patching up a Victoria 'Firefly' that had come off second best after colliding with a coalman's dray at the Hallesches Tor, an accident black spot even then. That done, I fetched down the order book to make a start on the accounts. It was a great time for the bike business! Everyone and his dog wanted to cycle, encouraged by the newspapers trumpeting the advantages: quicker journeys to work, fresh air, exercise, speedier deliveries, sporting competitions, an improved social life... I had my work cut out just keeping on top of the novelties – roll chains for pin-and-link, pneumatic tyres, three-speed gears, folding bikes for the army and lighter frames for women and youngsters.

It was only when I glanced in the mirror that I noticed her waiting. Joseph must have left the light on because having seen me working in the back, she had tried the door which, thank God, he hadn't locked. I remember checking my hands were clean before going to find out what it was she wanted.

Falling in love is like cresting a hill: freewheeling, a roaring in the ears, speed-blur to right and left, hair wind-rinsed, gravity unable to make up its mind whether to hold you down, or let you soar like a cork from a bottle of *Sekt*.

That was happiness, but being young I didn't know about sealing the memory, making it airtight. I thought it would last for ever. There has to be more. List her likes: tarot, faith healers, fortune-tellers, fakirs, mesmerists, clairvoyants...She liked the paraphernalia – cabinets, candles, incense, wax dolls. She liked to hold hands in the dark, to feel scared, to wonder 'what if,' to mock, to peer into the unknown. She liked the people – true believers, sceptics, con artists, charlatans, crazies, weirdoes. She liked having fun. That was Frieda.

5

But just as I think I am losing myself in remembering Frieda, I think of Claudia Hoffmann. Or rather of Sandra, standing at the door, needing all the strength in her free arm to hang on to a truculent, swollen-eyed Freddy. Both of them seemed surprised to see me and my assorted luggage, so much so that for a moment I wondered whether the summons to Tivoli had arisen from a misunderstanding. Then Claudia, disturbed by the departing roar of the car, came down to greet me, a black shawl thrown carelessly across her shoulders and wearing the confused, disoriented look of someone just woken from a nap.

We took tea in the *Vermeer-Zimmer* while I waited for Hoffmann to return. Crossing the floor still felt like treading on a giant chess board and while the window casements and heavy brocade curtain were no doubt perfectly authentic, Claudia herself looked out of place – it might have helped had she been wearing a turban and holding a pewter jug or arranging a basket of flowers.

I sipped my tea and tried to make conversation, 'Remember Bertorelli's,' I asked inconsequentially, 'when you were cross with me for eating the whole bowl of Turkish delight?'

But she was in no mood for small talk.

'Don't you *ever* worry about damnation?'

The ferocity of the question took me aback.

She picked up a guitar (another of Hoffmann's props) and began strumming listlessly. 'Why do people like me have to take on so much guilt, while others' (she meant me) 'sail through life without a care in the world?'

My feeling was if you can't accept the Catholic doctrine, don't join. But her lessons with Father had stalled at a crucial hurdle, the leap of faith. He had compared her to a child desperate to be able to swim but lacking the courage to enter the water. Dante had nothing to say on the matter, apparently.

She glanced at my copy of *Light Beyond Death's Shadow* on the coffee table – I must have left it behind – then said, 'Do you really believe we're not responsible for our feelings?'

'We needn't be ashamed of them, certainly. It all depends on what kind of higher being you believe in. For all I know the more you suffer the more you'll be compensated. Instead of fixating on sin, why not let in the light.'

As I said this, it was occurring to me that her indignation about responsibility didn't come from reading *Light From Beyond Death's Shadow*, but from a letter I had written to Alma Goerdeler while I was staying in Tivoli. "We have reached the closing chapter of our journey," I had told her, "we have reached the terminus which is acceptance. We are not responsible for our feelings. Now, if as you suggest, you wish to continue our friendship, it should be on a new footing..."

She must have been looking over my shoulder while I wrote the letter, crept up on me in those pumps of hers. But I never got the chance to challenge her because at that moment Sandra came in to say Hoffmann was back and was ready to see me. This time I remembered to take the book with me.

6

De Kuyper had stuck a cigar between his lips and, mislaying the cutter among his papers, bit the end off with his teeth, so that tobacco juice leaked from his lips. 'I see you're interested in our travelling exhibition.'

I was intrigued by some gaudily coloured prints that had been glued to the walls of the office to make a comic strip, like Busch's Max and Moritz. There was an uber-green field sprinkled with dandelions and daisies, rosy-cheeked lasses in folk dresses, a gent in a suit demonstrating some new fangled farm implement to a bemused country bumpkin. The panels were arranged in pairs: throwing away manure – bad; spreading it over the land – good; a metal plough was better than a wooden one. There was a winnowing machine you could harness to your horse.

These were advance notices for the travelling exhibition which was to spread the word that the government's agricultural reforms would benefit all. The circus was coming to town it seemed: Petrushka puppets, Magic Lantern shows, free tractor rides for the youngsters... Whatever it took to hold the peasants' imagination.

I would see De Kuyper driving around the estate in a pony and trap. On the Friday he offered to take me for a ride. I would have preferred to poke about a bit unsupervised, ask the way to the village, find a pub, but that was before I had experienced the boundlessness of the Steppe. As we rattled down "the Broadway", he pointed out the railway spur leading to the grain silos, the brick works, the vodka distillery, the new village school, the cottage hospital.

Kolya clearly had a vision. He was the sort who not only conceived of a thing, but made it happen. No wonder the villagers took his death badly.

When I collected these thoughts for de Kuyper, his reaction surprised me.

'He was forced into it, I mean into breaking off his studies in Italy. There was a crisis. The *moujiks* were on the rampage – looting, stealing, burning records, refusing to pay their rent...

It took guts to stand up to them, I'll say that for your friend. Ask Geronty, he was there. Of course he had the army to back him up.'

When he talked about the *moujiks* it was as if they were a force of nature, like the weather – something to be wary of, tamed.

'The *moujiks* must feel your breath on their necks. I said to Geronty, "The fellow before me, you gave him the run around." What I say to them is: "I can see through you and three feet under you".'

It occurred to me that de Kuyper had been drinking.

They had their own way of looking at things. For example a wall mirror in the master bedroom had dropped to the floor and smashed to smithereens, they said without human intervention (the maid swore to it). This was the week before they received the news of Kolya's death. They were still in a funk when I came on the scene and de Kuyper had to drive the Mogul himself just to prove there was no curse attached.

Another thing, there had been a change in their attitude towards me; they were becoming noticeably more deferential. I no longer had to go to the kitchen for breakfast but was waited on in the dining room.

When I told de Kuyper about this, he found it hilarious, 'They put two and two together and made five.'

A rumour had spread that I was to take over Grankino. The fact that I was hard of hearing and German only added to the credibility of this tale.

We made a stop outside a lock-up that served as a warehouse. There was something de Kuyper wanted to show me. We picked our way through machinery and farming equipment to a stack of packing crates. He broke one open with a crowbar and invited me to take a look. Whatever was inside was swaddled in straw and layers of tissue paper. Seeing me hesitate, he took the topmost object and handed it to me.

'Unwrap it - go ahead.'

It was a toy whistle shaped like a wooden bird. The way it had been hand-painted, the delicacy of the brushstrokes, the attention to detail had a strange effect on me. As I held it in my hand, I felt a connection to the maker; there was an understanding between us.

'Keep it for when you get back. It'll be worth a bob or two.' This was because the boy apprentices had been trained by two brothers, well-known artist friends of Kolya's, down from St Petersburg for the summer.

I said, 'There must be a business plan lying around somewhere – lists of people to contact, shipping agents, potential stockists, that kind of thing.'

'Something written down – are you kidding? Konradi kept it all up here.' He pointed to his temple. De Kuyper's predecessor, another friend of Kolya's had been in charge of the project before he 'buggered off to America' leaving him in the lurch. 'Never let a fellow turn your head.'

Turn your head – a strange thing to say.

When I asked what was in the other crates I was told more of the same – carved objects, also some ceramics, all originally destined for Paris. Kolya had been testing the market and was convinced there was money to be made from the wealthier patrons of the visiting Russian ballet which had been a great hit with the public. Like Chinoiserie in the eighteenth century, I supposed, or Hokusai drawings.

This kind of speculation was no help to de Kuyper, 'So tell me, what am I to do with it all?'

I said I would write to Hoffmann about it.

7

I must have been nine or ten when Kolya asked me if I would like to spend the summer holidays with him in Russia. Like boys do, I said 'yes' immediately, without thinking and I hoped with enough enthusiasm to convince him that we had struck an agreement he could not go back on. I had gone on to ask, a little shamefacedly, 'What is Grankino exactly?'

There was a park – he had told me that much, and 'grounds'. I suspected he was being modest in his use of the term and, fired by the stories of the Brothers Grimm, I imagined a forest where wild boar roamed but also elves and goblins, ogres and wizards. A park on the other hand implied gates, boundary walls and trees in manageable quantities – big climbable trees with roots like trip wires and bark we could break off or strip away to carve our names on with a penknife. There would be shadowy, more unkempt corners for playing hide and seek, where we could make strange noises as loud as we liked before cooling off in a waterfall like the one in Viktoria Park. There might even be a stream where we could fish for 'tiddlers'.

Nothing had prepared me for the reality: the Steppe stretching towards a horizon that seemed just another constant. The clouds dawdled, sometimes stopping dead in their tracks as if the challenge of crossing the sky had become too much for them. On the Steppe a crossroad was an event, a fold or hump in the countryside, a landmark. Occasionally something would move – a hare bounding across a field or a buzzard on the wing, otherwise... stillness. The only trees were willows down by the stream.

Another surprise about Grankino was the house. I had been expecting an ancestral pile, flunkies, a ballroom, marble columns at the very least. Actually the Konradis lived quite modestly in a single storey, clapperboard manor house, painted lime green, with a veranda and a weathervane in the shape of a cockerel. Only later did I realise where this misconception came from.

I had tried the communicating door between my bedroom and Kolya's and finding it unlocked, took a peep inside. It led to a dressing room which was positively *gemütlich* after the bedroom. I took off my shoes and weighed myself on the scales. I decided to try on Kolya's dressing gown and found a pair of nail scissors in one of the pockets. Thinking it wouldn't be missed I took it as keepsake. I was returning the dressing gown to the hook on the wall when, looking up, I saw it: the toy theatre we had played with as youngsters, on top of a cupboard gathering dust. Everything was still intact – the stage with its wooden frame, the painted scenery you could change according to the performance. There was a curtain made out of chintz which could be raised or lowered, a trap door, even an orchestra pit with footlights made out of tiny candles. Some actor figures had survived, made of cardboard with wires attached to the backs so you could move them around after pinning on the relevant costumes. I took out a handkerchief and wiped the dust away from the cardboard surface, this way, that way and realized that this was how I imagined Grankino – red drapes, a chequered floor, a marble staircase.

Kolya chose the plays which were inspired at first by Italian fairy tales. There was a pirate type called the Capitano and a clown, Arlecchino. Then Kolya brought along a book of illustrated tales from Pushkin – *The Golden Cockerel* was one, and *Tsar Saltan* – that was a favourite with both of us as my mother had read the story to me at home.

But I always had the feeling that he was caught up in drama of his own, something much closer to home, something from his own life. For example, he would introduce characters I had never come across in books – gossipy people with odd names – Petronella, Mrs Nilus, Nicolette, Alina, Sofya Petrovna. On these occasions, Kolya would pin dresses on the male characters – even the Capitano – and make them dance about the stage as if they were ballerinas. The way they moved and the things they said would send me into fits of giggles. And then, suddenly it would all come to an end, and always in the same way: "Alina" would storm on to the stage and scream at the top of her voice, 'Why am I always mopping up after the little retard?'

ST PETERSBURG

1

I keep having the same dream. I am on a journey without knowing exactly where I am heading. It makes me uneasy. Again and again I return to the same starting point. I am not alone, but who is with me? A woman. Frieda? Where are we? Italy more often than not. It might be the Arco di Riccardo, or Freitas's cemetery, or Brera – the courtyard in the art gallery. One constant – we are always being followed by a shadowy figure in black who I take to be a Jesuit.

The first time I had the dream, I cried out in my sleep and in my confusion patted the bedclothes where I expected to find Strammer Max. But I was not at home. I was in St Petersburg, a room in Pension Ritterhelm, on the Nevsky Prospekt. Cushioning my head with my hands I gazed up at the scallop pattern round the light fitting.

"It isn't fair on Frau Winter," Gerda had written in her last letter. If I didn't come home soon, they would have to find someone else to look after him. I imagined how the conversation would go between the two of them.

Frau Winter: The thing is, he won't stop barking; not only that, he won't let me get near my own sideboard – it's as if he's guarding it.

Gerda: Poor thing must be missing him.

Frau Winter: That must be it. Well, it has been a long time...He used to be so affectionate and playful; intelligent too, not like some dogs I know.

Bored with this scenario, I shunted Gerda and Frau Winter down the track to make way for sweet-shop Lisa, Frau Winter's not unattractive daughter, segueing to the harem girl with the white belly from Fanucci's studio, the heiress in the Austrian film who proved surprisingly adept at striking provocative poses for the cameraman, and (my own composition) Lindstrom's calendar girl gamely stripping down to her undies for a private viewing...

2

And there, materialising at the foot of the bed like the angel spirit in *Light Beyond Death's Shadow, was...* 'Jesus, Zoya!'

'Malingerer! What's the matter, aren't you glad to see me?'

I raised myself up on my elbows while she attacked the curtains, flooding the room with light.

What a hole was not a kind way to talk about Pension Ritterhelm – "not dear for St Petersburg and conveniently located on the main avenue" – but then Zoya had booked herself into the Astoria.

She was even more beautiful than I remembered, less Henny Porten now I came to think of it and more *die Asta* – Asta Nielsen in *The Abyss*, the scene where she does the tango with the gaucho.

Reaching out to bring her closer, I just managed to graze a firm, muscular buttock with my right hand. The silk dress, and her corset-less figure, showed her assets off to the full.

'Get dressed. We have to get a move on.'

We were going out then.

She disappeared behind the wardrobe door just long enough for me to pick up the empty beer bottle from the night table and smuggle it under the bed.

'I told you to throw this old jacket away,' she said before draping a dark suit and my only clean white shirt over the back of a chair; and while she was distracted with collars and ties, I slipped the Blue Book under the covers.

3

That would have been my first encounter with Domeniques. After one, the place was packed and it was while we were waiting in line that I had the sensation of *déja vu*, the eerie feeling that I had been in just such a queue, while being unable to pin down anything concrete, even if the downstairs dining room did remind me of the Moritzplatz branch of Aschinger's, the one with the arches.

Eventually they found us a table in the central aisle. I handed the menu to Zoya and excused myself to obey a call of nature. When I got back, she was nowhere to be seen and what I took to be our table was now occupied by strangers! Another dream? I counted the tables and hovered, getting in the way of a waiter carrying a tray at shoulder height. Was I the wrong side of the arches? It was like the time I came out of the public lavatory by the wrong door and panicked because I couldn't find my mother...

Then I saw Zoya waving from a booth by a window. We would be able to hear ourselves better there, she explained, and there was a view of the colonnade of the Kazan cathedral. I wonder now whether this was the real reason.

She really was *traum schön*, quite sensational. The Tulle veil, she let fall from time to time, made her smile mysterious, but what really suited her was the dress: grey and quite plain until a shaft of sunlight caught the gold flecks on the sleeves and bodice. When I complimented her on her outfit, she said it was the "English marchioness look"; she had lifted it from the cover of a society magazine.

'Guess what?' she said lolling her tongue in her cheek. 'I got the sack from Tirriochi's, how about that?'

There had been an argument about a wedding dress – during the "try on" a strip of lace had torn when the bride-to-be had stepped on it with the heel of her shoe. Zoya had assumed the bride's mother would pay for the extra fitting. One thing led to another, Zoya refused to apologise and, reluctantly, Madame gave her her cards.

'What will you do now?'

'There's no great hurry, *n'est pas*?'

She had an appointment at *Vienna Chic* later that afternoon.

That would have been the moment to set out my business proposition, "Cycles and Accessories for Ladies". I should have told her how I felt, told her how she made me feel. Things might have turned out differently. I lost my chance.

She had planted her elbows provocatively on the table, her chin resting on those nimble fingers of hers. 'We're going to have fun, you and I.'

4

I once saw a film where to show the passage of time, the pages on a calendar seemed to fall away like leaves in autumn. That was how it felt to be with Zoya in Petersburg, before things started to go wrong.

It was the season of White Nights when everyone heads for the Islands. Usually we rode the steamer although the first time Zoya insisted on hiring a Victoria "with pneumatic tyres for a smoother ride". That set me back eight rubles, not including the tip for the driver, but by then I had thrown caution to the winds.

'Will you be staying long?' I asked as we finished our dinner on the veranda of Dacha Ernst.

'That depends,' she said, playing with the folds of her napkin. 'I was thinking...if I did stay on I could be useful. You're going to need an interpreter and help with translating. Why don't you suggest it to Hoffmann?'

To my amazement we got away with it – Hoffmann agreeing to add her name to the pay roll as my assistant. (She had stood over me while I composed the letter.)

Zoya took her duties seriously at first, she wanted to know how I was getting on with *The Life*.

The Life of Pyotr Ilych Tchaikovsky by Modest Ilych Tchaikovsky ran to more than six hundred pages even in the abridged German edition and was heavy going with its musical quotations and lengthy extracts from family correspondence. This was the thick black tome Hoffman had given me at the same time as Kolya's diary.

'I'm surprised Kolya doesn't crop up more often,' I said. 'He is there at first – in the chapters about Italy, how charming Kolya was, his curiosity, his illnesses, but then it sort of tails off.'

'So, tell me about Klin.'

She had read one of my letters then.

Where to start? Whenever I think of Klin, galoshes come to mind because I was wet through and had a cold – I'd bought a miniature brandy at the station bar, Baku firewater with an oil derrick on the label, silhouetted black on yellow.

I notice that, writing Klin up for Gerda, I scrubbed out the rain altogether, describing instead the fields with cornflowers and dandelions, the pines and dripping birch trees, long grass, the scent of summer.

"Pyotr Ilych was a great one for walking, Kot said – every day without fail, before breakfast and after lunch, no matter what the weather. Kot had showed me the little table overlooking the park where the composer had liked to copy out scores or go over his manuscripts. Nature was an inspiration, Kot said. The house was bigger than I'd imagined, three storeys, painted lilac with fancy woodcarving around the eaves and windows."

Zoya was rolling her own cigarette. I watched her run her tongue along the folded edge of the paper, pinching off the surplus twists of tobacco with her fingernails, and returning them to the tin.

'Everything was exactly the way Tchaikovsky left it. I mean exactly – spectacles, gloves, slippers, even his hat boxes.'

'Like a museum.'

'More like a shrine where people come to pay their respects – it's as if he was Bach or Beethoven.'

'It's nothing to do with the music, it's chauvinism, they know a great Russian patriot when they see one.'

"A great Russian patriot" – the expression sounded familiar, but at the time I couldn't place it.

5

Domeniques was also where Zoya first remarked on the Baron's wristwatch. I slipped it from my wrist and showed it to her.

She made her "I'm impressed" face. 'Cartier, I don't think I've seen one of those before – not on a man, at least. You've been treating yourself.'

If she had only known!

The moment "Simplicissimus" left, the atmosphere in the Caffè Greco had changed for the better. With exaggerated courtesy, the Baron rose to his feet, gave me a long appraising look, then shook me firmly by the hand. More than firmly, his handshake was crushing, belying a faux-gentle, almost sentimental demeanour. Now Molly too, after adding a few touches to his makeup with the aid of a compact mirror, seized my hand and pulled me down beside him.

'Isn't it beastly of him, leaving a girl in the lurch like that, and without a penny to live on?' He patted me consolingly on the knee, as if I too had been thrown over.

He was talking nineteen to the dozen so I caught little of what he said until he showed me his purse with a few *soldi* in it and a single crumpled 10 lire note. I took this to mean that he was on the point of leaving and drained my *corretto*. But the Baron had ordered two double shots of grappa and Molly's departure allowed him to move to my side of the table. As he sat there, beaming at me like a toy soldier, I was struck by one of Zoya's maxims, "If he's in worsted, he's a gentleman". She would also have approved of the mauve handkerchief unfolding from the top pocket of his suit, and the matching socks.

Then he ruined the effect with a crass opening gambit, 'I suppose you rely on servants a good deal – to run the bath, answer the door and so forth?'

My impediment wasn't as severe as all that, I explained.

His mouth formed a non-committal, 'Ah'.

He sidled a little closer on the pretext of showing me the magazine the aesthetes had been poring over before they left with "Simplicissimus". I was beginning to feel uncomfortable and loosened my collar, which he took in quite the wrong way. Giving my biceps a squeeze, he wanted to know if I "boxed at all". 'You have the build of a pugilist. You would give the other fellow a bloody nose without the shadow of a doubt.'

To change the subject I commented on his wristwatch, the first one I had seen. He threw me a reproachful look, but unclasped it and placed it daintily in my hand. A Santos Dumont, he explained,

Santos Dumont was an aviator and a personal friend of Cartier's.

It was then that he squeezed my thigh, his bony fingers like crab pincers. I pulled him off and said he was taking a fucking liberty and that if he didn't keep his hands to himself, I would kick up a fuss and call for the manager. He pleaded with me to calm down, he didn't mean to cause offence.

No. Time to go. As I got to my feet he tugged at my jacket, but I made a break for the main door. Outside I almost collided with Molly who must have left something behind. It was not until I reached the end of Via Condotti and was breathing regularly that I realised the Baron had slipped his watch into my pocket.

For days afterwards, I could not look at the watch without being reminded of that damned Baron slavering in my ear. I considered getting rid of it, but it was too valuable to throw away. On the other hand, if I sold it, what if the baron had second thoughts and demanded it back? For all I knew he may have reported it stolen and left the details with the police. They would be on to me straight away. For the same reason, I couldn't risk taking it to a pawnbroker's. I considered posting it to Caffè Greco, but how could I be sure one of the waiters wouldn't get to it first?

6

Zoya said, 'If it's a limited edition, I should get it insured right away. You were saying – about Klin? You were there to snoop around presumably, looking for clues.'

I wondered where she was heading with this line of questioning and played safe by telling her about the photograph on the chimneypiece next to the marble clock. Here was a very young Kolya, kitted out in a velvet-collared jacket I didn't recognise, knickerbockers and a straw hat that seemed glued to the back of his head. He had a "little boy lost" look, and in keeping with an arranged composition, his hand was planted carefully on Modest Ilych's shoulder. Both Tchaikovsky brothers were sitting, but the fourth man in the picture, a youth, was standing almost side-on to the camera; there was a cockiness about him that suggested that he had come up with this particular idea himself, even insisted on it.

'Where was the picture taken?' Zoya asked.

'San Remo.' The show-off in the photograph was the valet, Sofronov. He could not have been more than sixteen, yet he was dressed exactly like the brothers – bowler hat, watch chain, walking stick.

Kot would have snatched it from my hands if I hadn't have handed it over voluntarily. It was his job as archivist and curator to look after the exhibits: "Leave it. That one belongs in the bedroom, it was a particular favourite of Cher Mâitre. Modest Ilych will return it to the proper place when he gets back."

'You keep saying "Kot"'

'That was his name.'

Zoya's laugh was like a burst of fire from a Maxim gun.

' "Herr Kot" You got that wrong.'

Kot was Russian slang for pimp.

I was on the point of moving on when Kot, or what ever his real name was, had called me to the window, "That's Sofronov."

I saw a middle-aged man having trouble with a key. Servants getting above themselves was nothing new, but this one was half-cut in the middle of the day.

Kot said, "He's been to the post office – funny how it takes some people."

I had done a stupid thing at Klin which was still bothering me. I decided to open up to Zoya about it.

'You *think* you signed the visitor's book?'

'I was supposed to be incognito.'

Remembering what Hoffman had told me about being discreet around these people, I had claimed to be a music salesman representing Breitkopf and Härtl – a Leipzig firm, I had done my homework, though not thoroughly enough. When "Kot" asked if he might have a visiting card, I was forced to bluff.

'What was wrong with saying you were Kolya's friend?'

A better question might have been, what was a man with a hearing problem doing in the music business.

7

Black River, the site of the duel that wasn't in the guidebook, was where Zoya read her poem – I say read, declaimed more like, giving it everything she had, the works. Not her poem, Pushkin's, because Pushkin was the one who fought the duel with the baron and ended up bleeding to death in the snow. The meadow had gone; in its place was a small park and, marking the spot, a plaster bust mounted on a pedestal. In Berlin there would have been a proper monument, like Schiller's outside the Konzerthaus. I found this all the more strange because the Russians don't just admire Pushkin, the way we Germans admire Goethe, he is in their blood. Pushkin is their common denominator, the one thing they can all agree on: the necessity for Pushkin.

Pointing to the red roses and carnations strewed at the base, Zoya said, 'Those are left by ordinary members of the public, and they're fresh.'

We walked on and she told me more about him – about the poetry mostly, and how it was always getting him into hot water with the authorities – a bit of a red by the sound of it. When she told me he had African blood I though she was having me on. But it was true, his grandfather came from Abyssinia and Pushkin himself had black curly hair and a dark skin.

We crossed the little bridge to Kamenny Island. I was reminded of Milan and our trips to the civic gardens. Zoya liked her outdoors tidy and decorous I noticed: a lily pond here, an ornamental bridge there, water untroubled enough to see your reflection in. It seemed strangely out of character, this fondness for tranquillity and ran counter to what little she had told me about her upbringing. Yet come to think of it, everything about her behaviour that day, starting with the poetry recital, was unlike anything I'd seen in Italy. Why was that?

I was still trying to figure it out when she said, 'When you wrote to tell me you were on your way to Russia I couldn't believe it. "What a gad about!" I thought.'

' "Seize the day", you advised.'

'But just like that.' (She snapped her fingers). 'One minute you're in Rome, the next it's off to Odessa. Banish trouble, banish care – forget the unpaid bills, the shop going to the dogs.'

'All taken care of.'

'Something turned up then, a development?'

'Estate business.'

'So you're a businessman now?'

'Errand boy more like, the friendly "postie" – pay's well though.'

'Well, that accounts for your time in the Ukraine. What brings you to Petersburg?'

'More of the same.'

'But you haven't given up on Kolya because you went to Klin. Odd, that you should worry about a little thing like signing the visitor's book...'

'Hoffman's instructions remember: "be discreet." '

'Klin was Hoffman's idea?'

'I didn't say that.'

'You inferred it.'

We carried on walking, so close now that the backs of our hands were touching, brushing, grazing. I counted the times – four, five and still she let it happen. I thought about how her skin would feel beneath the gauze of her blouse. It had been a long time...

'So, what's the latest theory? You still believe Kolya was lured to Trastevere?

'Let's put it this way, I don't think it was chance.'

'But not by one of our lot, surely, I've already explained...'

'Actually it was you who put me on to it with that press cutting.'

'Press cutting?'

'You remember – "Dateline Trieste. Espionage Ring." '

Clearly she had no idea what I was talking about. But as I was on a roll, I gave her the gist so she could follow my train of thought.

'Kolya was spying on the *Austrians*? Are you missing your top storey?'

'It would explain the medal – and his friendship with that cadet…'

'Oh, so you think officer cadets go around with blueprints for the new generation of battleship in their trouser pockets? Kolya liked to travel. You've been reading too many mystery stories – people in railway carriages suspecting their fellow passengers are up to no good.'

'Or promenading on the deck of a ship,' I added, thinking of Kolya and Barkov. Put like that, though it did sound far fetched. 'Got any better ideas?'

'The Modest Ilych angle sounds promising…'

'So far as it goes; I told you, Kolya barely gets a mention in *The Life* after they get back from Italy.'

'And until Kolya came of age, Modest Ilych was still…'

'*In loco parentis.*'

'Then doesn't it follow they were living in the same house? You need to fill in the gaps. Find out who their friends were, who they hung out with. But start with the Address Office – the records go back years, the police insist on it. What is he doing nowadays?'

'Modest Ilych? You mean how does he earn a living? Search me. He wrote a libretto for Rachmaninov but that was years ago. Did you know Rachmaninov plays tennis?'

'A libretto did you say? Then, start with the Conservatory – and go as Theo Brand, cut out the cloak and dagger stuff.'

8

Dacha Ernst again. I was still "having fun", wasn't I?

The couple at the neighbouring table had got up to join the others dancing under the paper lanterns. Zoya turned around to see what I was looking at, then nodded from side to side, out of time with the music.

She went back to eating her dessert – a sorbet. I watched her scoop the ice from the silver cup, swallow, lick her lips.

I said, 'I still say Modest Ilych was leaving Kolya out of the story on purpose. He only gets a few mentions – well, so far – and I'm well into it.'

Spoon, scoop, swallow…

'Don't you agree?'

'How would I know, when you won't let me see it? Look, you yourself said he gets a lot of mentions early on, so what's the big deal?'

Every so often her eyes would slide to the left, as if there was something a lot more interesting just out of view.

'Why are you pretending to be dense this evening – is it just to annoy me?'

'Now who's being dense. The book isn't about Kolya, it's the biography of an important composer. Kolya not being musical might have something to do with it. I could eat another one of those.'

She was fond of desserts, gobbled them up; yet she never put on weight.

As if reading my mind, she said, 'You're putting on weight again. When did you last look at yourself side on in the mirror? It's those roasts at Pension Ritterhelm, I don't know how you have the stomach for them, and in this weather.'

Instinctively I drew in my abdomen but she was right, I had been overdoing it. It wasn't the dinners, it was the beer.

'Going back to Modest Ilych – it's his version of events from start to finish. What are you expecting, the unvarnished truth? Try reading between the lines.'

She was sketching now – doodling rather on the back of a flier. Another hat, piled up with artificial fruit. English ladies would be wearing this style in the coming season, she predicted. At the Ascot races it would be *comme il faut*.

We started to argue over the English equivalent, whether you said 'the done thing' or 'quite the thing'. In truth I couldn't have cared less but she could be very obstinate and the exchanges became rather heated. In the end I let her have the last word, as usual.

The regular waiter was clearing away the empty dishes before we ordered coffee. He was still hovering over the table when a colleague arrived with a single red rose wrapped in tissue paper; with it was a note, which Zoya duly read. I followed her gaze to a table two rows away, on the far side of the duckboard. Seated there were three or four hilarities-in-a-bottle, all dressed alike in green tunics and looking very smug. One of them had already asked her to dance.

I made a grab for the note but Zoya was too quick for me. I laughed, shook my head, threw an arm over the back of the chair, gestures I hoped might convince my audience of fellow diners that I was making light of it, that the attention only showed what a fine taste in women I had, that I could take a joke as well as the next man; knowing full well that it was Zoya's reaction they were all waiting for. She didn't acknowledge them. She didn't have to. Her heart was galloping off without her, any fool could see that: her cheeks glowed like coals stirred into life with a poker.

I was determined to put a stop to it. 'Send it back with the waiter – or tear it up. Keep the rose if you like.'

'It's just a game,' she said, playing with the corners of her napkin – 'a dare.'

'Who are they? What's that uniform?'

'They're guardsmen.'

'They can't be – they're too young.'

They were cadets from the Corps des Pages, the top officer training school.

I said, 'You *have* gone over to the other side.'

'I know which one my bread is buttered on, if that's what you mean. Now can we change the subject?'

She kissed me on the cheek. But any pleasure I had been taking from her company vanished like air expelled from the teat of a balloon. I felt backed into a corner. But what to do – leave? That would be playing into their hands. A ridiculous thought entered my head: that the situation was like Pushkin at Black River when he was provoked into fighting a duel. I had to pull myself together, act as if nothing had happened.

'Freitas said working in a bike shop made me a petty-bourgeois.' This had rankled at the time and was still bugging me.

'You're not a Marxist. So why let it bother you?'

Petty-bourgeois ranked pretty low in the pecking order, I was sure about that.

'You're right, I'm not a Marxist but "I know which side my bread is buttered on". You won't find me cosying up to the coal barons.'

'What's brought this on?'

'People like him think I'm stupid, that I've never heard of Bebel, Kautsky and the rest.'

'I think you're missing the point...'

'You don't need to study Karl Marx or the Russians. It's all there in the newspapers.' She had reduced me to behaving like a schoolboy volunteering an answer – so determined was I to justify myself, my right to a point of view on the subject. 'Ask me about the Moabit Riots. Go on.'

It had begun, with the lock-out at Kupfe and Co and Stinnes bringing in blackleg labour; the police had trampled the garden allotments out of spite and beat the English journalists black and blue with the flats of their swords. And I'd read the other side of the story from the *Berliner Tageblatt*: Chancellor Bethmann's speech in the Reichstag, the SPD disowning the thugs (rent-a-mob from Stettin) for throwing coal and beer bottles, or scattering crockery in the path of the horses. Freitas wasn't the only one who could put both sides of an argument.

'What wasn't in the papers,' she said, 'was the driving force, the dynamo that made the wheels turn.'

She meant History with a capital H.

I shrugged and left it to Zoya to break the silence.

'I bought a bicycle.'

I didn't believe that for a minute. 'Really? What make?'

'The one you recommended.'

She was bluffing. I knew it.

'Did you ask for the hygienic saddle?'

I had to explain the joke again. Back in the '90s a GP, concerned that women might be getting the wrong kind of pleasure from cycling, had come up with the idea of a saddle with a groove in the centre to avoid... "Numbness", he said.

I suggested hiring bicycles so that we could go riding together.

She pulled a face, 'Not in this heat – besides, I don't have the attire.'

'"Attire." You mean bloomers,' I said, shaking a dollop of scorn from the bottle. 'You don't know how to ride a bike, that's the real reason.'

She arched her eyebrow in a way I didn't much care for.

'It's not so hard when you get the hang of it – and you have a good teacher.'

'You want me to ask who?' My stomach heaved. It was the feeling of being in a lift when it drops a couple of floors without warning. 'You're going to tell me anyway.'

Leopardi, from the craft shop.

9

Every moment I had to myself, when Zoya was visiting the hairdresser, or shopping, or having her portrait taken at Bulla's, or on assignment for *Vienna Chic,* I spent poring over the entries in the Blue Book. It was clever of Kolya to come up with a code that only deaf people would recognise. He had always enjoyed brain busters and would bring his *500 Curious Puzzles and Paradoxes* into school to torture me with the Case of the Dishonest Jeweller or the Entangled Scissors.

It was the day when Zoya and I were supposed to take off for the Baltic coast (Konnaya Lakhta) that I made a new discovery. I had been looking forward to our trip to the seaside, but when I got up that morning I was disappointed to see that the weather had turned misty and a fine rain was falling. On top of that there was a note under my door from Zoya: something had cropped up, an appointment she had forgotten about, and we would have to meet later than planned, not at Mars Field but at the Novaya Derevnya tram stop. Relieved that she wasn't crying off altogether, I got down to the serious business of decoding.

When the maid, smelling pleasantly of the laundry cupboard, arrived to clean the room, I collected my things, including the Blue Book and found a place to sit in the theatre gardens. It was still overcast but the rain had more or less stopped.

There was an entry in the book that had been puzzling me for some time, one I had trouble deciphering: "A.S., Campo dei Fiori," followed by a run of deaf symbols. The first I recognised almost immediately as "talk". Kolya had had a talk with this A.S. A "bad" talk, bad in the sense of unpleasant possibly. The other symbols around A.S. were more bothersome; but I kept at it and managed to decipher something about clashing or coming up against. A "confrontation"? Had Kolya had a confrontation with A.S. over... "a letter"? But who was this A.S? Perhaps if I was to write to Hoffmann...

When I next looked at my watch, I realised I had left it far to late to get to Novaya Derevnya. I ran back to the hotel, took the stairs rather than join the queue for the lift, only to find that the maid had locked the door with my room key inside.

Twenty minutes later and the tram had got no further than Trinity Bridge. I willed it on as it trundled across the Neva and onto Bolshoy Prospekt where the driver was able to gather speed and we surged forward.

I traced 'A.S.' absentmindedly on the smeared glass and became lost in the sheer repetition of the houses and apartments which passed like a refrain: every door, a bell pull and brass plate, bell pull and brass plate....

Alyosha Sofronov – A.S. At Klin there were two names on the

front door, Sofronov and Tchaikovsky.

Now all I could see through the window were pine trees and the odd dacha. I had missed my stop and was completely lost. There was no way I was going to meet up with Zoya. I turned to my neighbour but could not get the words Novaya Derevnya to come out right. I was sure now that we had passed the stop and jumped up to tug the bell, a reflex action that made my neighbour cringe, as if he was expecting me to belt him. I must have been talking too loud because they threw me off before I had the chance to ask the way.

10

The letter clenched in my fist, I sat scowling at the green mantel clock. It glowered straight back at me, defiantly and with malice, the way a cat does.

"Heinrich has asked me to marry him."

Marry? *Marry*, what was she talking about?

My first thought – but he's on tour; as if there was a law stating that proposals of marriage had to be delivered in person! Heinrich now, not Heini – inferring respect, consideration, *subordination*. What had gotten into her? She used to lampoon him: "Hymie" Reuss our little joke – galling.

"My last chance," she pleaded, "Too late now for children I know, but...Please write and tell me what you think."

What I thought!

We had arrived at Frau Tarasova's 'on spec', Zoya furious with me for not making an appointment. We were shown into the front parlour where there were magazines on the table like at the dentist's, but instead of Novocaine and mouthwash it reeked of sticky sweet flowers.

I showed Zoya the postmark. 'Two weeks for a letter – that can't be right.'

She said, 'Welcome to Russia.'

They censored letters, it was the same with the newspapers, the foreign editions delivered to hotels – inked out lines, sometimes whole paragraphs. There was a special term for it, "perlustration". If a letter wasn't stuck down properly they used a long, reed-like stick to loosen the adhesive. Otherwise they steamed it open. Sealing wax didn't deter them either because they had duplicate stamps. They didn't open every letter of course – you had to be on a 'watch list' to qualify.

The maid was back to give us the brush off. Madame Tarasova received visitors from 2-4pm of a Tuesday and said to come back then.

Madame Tarasova had been on my to-do list for some time, but I kept her to myself after Zoya had caught me with the Blue Book and almost wrenched it from my hands. It was on the inside back cover that I had found the note and I had almost missed it as it was written faintly in pencil: "Bryullova, now Tarasova (!)" followed by a street name in St Petersburg. Pencil suggested precaution, details that could be erased at a later date, while the exclamation mark might be a reaction to... a change in her circumstances. Was there more to it than that? An entanglement, an affair? It was worth following up, at any rate, the woman might know something.

I had asked Zoya to come along because she knew the Address Office on Sadovaya where they gave out house numbers and I fobbed her off with an excuse that we were visiting an acquaintance of Modest Ilych. She was grouchy, because the day before she'd had to spend several hours with me at a police station applying for a bicycle permit. I reminded her that she was now "on the payroll" and strictly speaking my employee. Besides, there was the possibility that this Madame Tarasova might only speak Russian.

11

By the time we set out for her place for the second time – at Zoya's insistence in a Victoria, she wouldn't hear of taking the 30 kopek tram – the sky had darkened dramatically and it was clear we were in for a storm. Lights were going on and I can remember smelling dust settling on the dampening pavement.

In the drawing room two youngish men in office clothes were hanging a painting. Madame, her back turned, was inspecting the picture from all angles and taking her time about it. A tan-and-black Pomeranian was scampering about struggling to gain a foothold on the marquetry floor. That the painting had a message for me alone, I only realised later.

I suspected the real reason Zoya was making me suffer was my behaviour following the Konnaya Lakhta mix-up. It had been two in the morning and I was pounding the door with my fists, yelling her name. A red-faced man in a dressing gown remonstrated with me but I was so worked up, so *enraged* she wasn't in, that I had to fight the urge to charge at it with my shoulder. What fuelled my jealousy, I now realise, was a Chekhov story I had been reading about a skirt-chaser and a bored wife on holiday at the seaside. I imagined Zoya being preyed on by just such a character, prowling the Baltic boardwalks. She finally got to bed at five she boasted, and had to wake the night porter.

It was all getting in the way – the unpleasantness over Konnaya Lakhta, Zoya making things difficult at the address office, the business with Reuss and Gerda – when what was needed more than ever just then was clear thinking, an *Aktionsplan* as the general staff would have put it.

I should have been making the introductions, stating our business but already Zoya was turning the conversation in the wrong direction. What made it more difficult was the way they hit it off: Zoya was "Karsavina to the very life" while she was in raptures over Madame's dress and so much at home that she felt free to "pinch the fabric". The "geisha look" Zoya told me afterwards, but to me it was a weird outfit with wide silk lapels, far too much lace and a cherry-coloured sash. Then we were back to Karsavina – a ballerina, not an actress as I had first supposed, and a regular at Madame's "Wednesdays" – never missed when she wasn't touring.

I brought across a black lacquer chair, so shiny I tested the surface to make sure the paint was dry, and set it at an angle best suited to follow the conversation. I was determined not to let Zoya steal what should have been my show. I tried intervening but the compliments were served and returned, lobbing the net like tame exchanges in ladies' tennis, leaving me like Rachmaninov's wife on the side-lines without a doubles partner. I could not get a word in edgewise so I left them to it.

"My last chance" Gerda had written in *that* letter. Where did that leave me with my side-line in bereaved women, the time wasted on séances, in tracking obituary columns? Either it was the angelic countenance they were after, or they were playing with the notion that deaf people were horny and oversexed. Where I had been on the wrong track was in assuming that I wouldn't, one day, have to give as well as take.

Madame had arranged herself on the chaise longue her left arm stretched languorously along the backrest, so that her legs were daringly crossed like the woman on a poster advertising cognac. When she flexed a white-stockinged foot as if considering how to show it off to best effect, she was more like the till girl in Tiriocchi's.

'Why is he still carrying his hat?'

I had her attention at last. I glanced at Zoya who knew my history with hats, in this case a straw boater I had christened "Bertrand", then said that I would prefer to hold on to it, if it was all the same to Madame. I sensed *Schadenfreude* around me like a magnetic field.

Even her worse enemy would have had to admit that there was enough about Madame Tarasova to suggest that she had turned a few heads in her day. But fashion houses and schools of deportment have no antidote for liver spots on the backs of hands or slack folds of skin under the jawline. I knew the type – the business with the foot for example, that was just like Frau Pechstein.

Frau Pechstein was one of that breed that gets hitched to stock certificates and insurance policies and whose grief at the demise of their elderly husband goes no further than the death column in the newspaper. The flirtation creeps in at first with small breaches in the mourning code – a dab of rouge, a white handkerchief, a fleeting glimpse of forearm, a scent more exotic than rosewater. Then once it has its foot in the door, while you are setting out the brochures or explaining the secret doctrine or altered states of existence, you notice the quickening intake of breath, the fingers worrying away at a wrist – signs that it is not consolation they are after, but fun and games.

I could torpedo Reuss with a single salvo if I had a mind to: "Why do you think he waited until I went away before coming-on to you? Because I know he's got previous in that department and if you don't believe me there are witnesses." I had recognised one of the girls from the Café Chantant in Moabit. Reuss had run across them in a night club – Minna and her friend. He was playing to the gallery as always with his magic tricks and drinking games.

By the time we left to go to Kellner's place around the corner (Reuss had the run of it for the weekend), both of them were so far gone that they weren't even spooked by the way it had been done up – black paint from ceiling to floor with gold stars. Minna already had that far away look when Reuss led her into the next room, leaving us to it. When he came back he was bollock naked apart from the opera cloak, while she was down to her stockings. The next thing I remember Minna was spread out on the settee, her head thrown back, her legs apart while he was probing her vulva with his fingers as if it was a doctor's examination. That was enough for my one who demanded to be taken home. "That's the kind of man Reuss is," I would say, "Case proven."

They had left the room to inspect more of Madame's fine things. I called the Pomeranian to me and picked her up. She had been well cared for – good teeth, a healthy coat – but it would have been considerate to lay a carpet.

I went to take a closer look at the painting. I learned afterwards that it showed an episode from Homer. There were people on the shoreline; a lank, purposeful woman at the front of what seemed to be a procession. She was clearly meant to be beautiful and was driving a chariot pulled – and this was the odd thing – by a donkey. Behind her, at a respectful distance, were her handmaids who appeared to be leading a dishevelled man, dressed in white and downcast, his hands joined, perhaps bound, as if he might be a prisoner. Curious to see how the artist had painted such a peculiar-looking sky, I stepped right up to the canvas, close enough to distinguish the individual flecks of silver, grey and purple paint – there was even a nicotine yellow in the mix.

Gerda was bluffing I decided; the thing with Reuss was a ploy to get me rattled, rattled enough to return home. The idea of her marrying *him* now struck me as comical. Reuss, of all people, with his spells and divinations and his place reeking of patchouli and sweaty bed linen. Gerda would never stand for it. I laughed out loud, terrifying the Pomeranian which I allowed to scamper across the floor barking.

Tea had been served before I finally had a chance to bring Kolya into the conversation. By now I noticed, Madame and Zoya were on first name terms, Zoya was calling her Helena. No, she couldn't recall Kolya mentioning any friend by the name of Brand. She did remember meeting Tobler on one occasion. That would have been...She directed all her answers at Zoya. I noticed she insisted on calling Kolya, "Nicky". Who was she then? An aunt? A governess? Then it occurred to me – the toy theatre: Alina then, not Helena – Madame Tarasova, as she now was, was Kolya's mother!

When I next caught up with the conversation, she was justifying herself to Zoya. Her worst mistake had been agreeing to entrust Kolya to that...I forget the epithet she used for Modest Ilych. So why did she?

She confided in Zoya, 'You know Konradi turned me out of my own home? Nicolas' father always thought he knew best... They were at school together, my former husband and Modest Ilych, both brothers as a matter of fact — The Imperial School of Jurisprudence. For some men it's enough.'

If she was to be believed, Modest Ilych also carried the can for the breakup of her marriage and her exclusion from Konradi's will.

Her version of events was as flawless as a carefully polished pebble, the inconsistencies smoothed out with sandpaper, the less plausible details rubbed at with soap and water until everything gleamed.

What I couldn't stomach was her icy self-possession. Less than half a year had passed since her only son had died a violent death yet she betrayed no emotion. But whatever I thought of her, she had meant a lot to Kolya. I told her about the toy theatre, about *Tsar Saltan* and the picnics.

She looked at me with genuine surprise.

'Picnics! They had taken my son, those doctors. He was no longer my son, do you understand what I am saying? I no longer recognised him. He wasn't the same.'

She had suffered a complete nervous collapse. If it hadn't have been for Bryullov she would never have got over it.

Then the picnics had been make believe. But she had given herself away.

I challenged her: 'A bit much though, for his own mother to call him a "little retard" '

Bad form they would have called it in her circles; for my father it would have been chutzpah. I think he would have approved.

12

Zoya followed half an hour later. It was only when I flagged down a cab that I realised I had scrunched my hat so badly that the crown had conflated into the brim. The storm had passed and the sun was beating down on the roof of the droshky. Zoya ordered the driver to lower the hood ('Be firm with them,' she said.)

She waited until we crossed Suvorov Square before she turned on me. 'What got into you? That was rude. If you can't follow the social norms, people will think you're an imbecile.'

'She called him a retard – a *retard*.'

'It was something in that letter wasn't it? What does Gerda want now?'

I hated the way she called her Gerda.

'*Ça me fait chier*, I thought it was women who made scenes! Children invent things...'

'Retard – you think he was making that up?'

'Maybe she'd had a hard day...'

'His mother?'

'Why not his mother? I bet your mother had a hard time.'

'My mother didn't run off with a fancy man,' I said. 'Tell the driver to take Voznesensky Prospekt.'

'You tell him. I thought we were going to Dominique's.'

'Not there again. Isn't there anywhere else?'

'You mean a beer parlour?'

'Beer *keller*. My mother wouldn't be seen in a dress like that. The geisha look, you said – with those boobs! She'd do better shopping off-the-peg in Manheim Brothers.' The clothes there were in regulation sizes, each with its own coloured star. Tarasova was a red for "ample".

'You've lost me.'

'*You* still haven't got over Konnaya Lakhta.'

'Konnaya Lakhta. What's there to get over?'

'Then why have you been avoiding me?'

'I'm here aren't I?'

'Why are you really here?' I realised I had been putting off that question, dreading the answer.

She took the easy way out: 'No reason. I like it here.'

I should have left it there but I had a grievance that was nagging at me, a scab I needed to pick at.

'She froze me out in there— and you let her.'

'If you'd have stayed, you would have learned something about the other husband, Bryullov.'

I didn't rise to the bait. 'What kind of a mother doesn't wear mourning?'

Where I came from, the rule for mourning was six months "full" followed by six months "reduced" for close family. When Pop died we did everything by the book, Mama wouldn't have had it any other way. I remember being kitted out in a black suit and being put in charge of sealing the envelopes for the invitations to the funeral "do", while Gerda saw to stopping the clock in the front room, covering the mirror and sticking the laurel wreath on the front door.

'You tried that on with me – the wearing black thing.'

'You weren't Kolya's mother. What else were you talking about behind my back?'

'This and that,' smiling to herself as she said it. 'The marriage market actually. She offered to find me a husband. She thought I could do better.'

'That's a lie.'

'Is it?' She showed me a card – an invitation to a party.

'You're not going?'

'Try stopping me.'

They had more in common than a taste for fine things I was coming to realise.

'After how she treated Kolya?'

'*I* don't owe Kolya anything. Look, she was in a bind. Women need permission from their husbands to travel abroad. It's the law here. No written consent, no passport. Now do you understand?'

'Are you blaming Konradi for objecting to her whoring around?'

'Charming.'

'You call that being a good mother?'

'Marriages break down, couples divorce. It's called real life. She found love elsewhere...'

' "She found love elsewhere" Where did you pick that up – in some trashy novel? Why not shack up in St Petersburg, if she was so desperate? Let me tell you something: she connived to get Kolya into that school. She did it to be with Bryullov.'

'Aren't you the moral one.'

'It's sickening.'

'What's sickening about a woman trying to live her own life? Stop being so... so damned Prussian.'

13

"And they brought unto Him one that was deaf and had an impediment in his speech. And He took him aside from the multitude, and put His fingers into his ears, and He spit, and touched his tongue, and looking up to heaven, He sighed and saith unto him, *Hephata*, that is, be opened. And straightway his ears were opened, and the string of his tongue was loosed, and he spoke plain."

That was why his mother had taken him to the priest, to be exorcised. The sudden onset of deafness in her son had spooked the peasants and they needed to be appeased.

Mark 7:34 was engraved on a wooden tablet and displayed prominently in Chateau Perache. Kolya had got into trouble after we had been assigned to make a drawing of the episode. While the rest of us focussed on Jesus as we were supposed, Kolya drew an odd figure with a head like a potato and an O for a mouth, from which poured a stream of demons (little green goblins), while another figure, with a black hat, spewed three arcing lines which, Kolya later explained to me, represented gob.

Were *we* to blame? They were willing to subject us to anything: I remember enduring mustard plasters, syringes, oil tipped from a burning spoon, salt to dislodge blockages of "foreign matter" –

but… an exorcist!

14

The repercussions following that business with the girls over at Kellner's place started with a visit from the *Schupo*. Somehow my one's brother had got wind of what we'd been up to – what Reuss had been up to – and reported us. They searched my room and took away some 'calling cards' I had printed for a bit of self-promotion ('Consultant in matters of the Occult' it said). Reuss should have been in a lot more hot water than I was, but lucky for him his girl stayed 'mum' and all they wanted from him was a statement. I learned through a third party that he had offered to appear for me as a character witness if the case came to court and I thought, thanks very much. They told me they were sending my papers to the prosecutor but as I was "not all there" and there was a backlog of cases involving "spirituals" I might get away with a fine which, *Gott Sei Dank* is what happened.

(Fortunately Gerda was away on a training course at the time and everyone agreed to keep *shtumm* about it when she got back.)

Gerda has got it into her head that it was she who first introduced me to Reuss after meeting him at a rehearsal with her choral society, forgetting that I knew him already from Hartmann's bookstore – still there on the corner of Kronenstrasse although it has seen better days. Hartmann's specialised in matters of the Occult and sold everything from *planchettes* and Ouija boards to horoscope charts, Tarot packs, do-it-yourself séance kits, as well as books and pamphlets. It was busiest during lunch hour, especially on Saturdays when people popped in on the way home from work. Some were enthusiasts, others came to titter – it was all the same to Hartmann who relished watching the scandalized minority, especially clergymen, hurrying past the display window, eyes averted.

My first encounter with Reuss was on just such a Saturday afternoon. I was in Hartmann's skim-reading Mrs Hope's new book and was drawn particularly to the photographs of "spectral figures becoming visible to the naked eye through ectoplasm, released by a medium in a state of trance." Mrs Hope was no longer in the news but I had seen her in her heyday at the Exhibition Park on Alt Moabit. Frieda had got us tickets – good seats, her mother knew someone who worked there. There were around a thousand people in the hall and it was so hot and stuffy that at one point someone fainted. What stands out in my memory about the evening though was a second disturbance when a woman at the back of the auditorium ran right past us and straight down the aisle. She was being chased by an usher and had got as far as the stage before another attendant tried to block her path. Mrs Hope though, beckoned to her, then helped her up onto the stage. Frieda had already explained that Mrs Hope had contacted a young sailor who had drowned at sea a few months earlier. The sailor, this woman was now insisting, was her son.

'Doctored – the photographs; an obvious hoax.' It was Reuss looking over my shoulder. He had a darkroom; photography was a hobby. He invited me to come with him to see how it's done.

Following his instructions, I struck a pose, imagining myself to be Moses pointing the chosen people in the direction of the Promised Land. I had to keep this up for fully five minutes by Reuss' stopwatch while he disappeared under the blanket to capture the shot. Then he photographed me again; this time seated, hands on lap. The trick was to superimpose one image on top of the other, using the two glass plates. Eh, voilà. As Reuss swilled the plate in the chemical bath, I saw myself and in the background a ghostly image of the prophet Moses.

Reuss was not denying there might be *something* to spirit photography in as much as a photographer, unlike a painter, is not in full control of the composition. In a photographic image odd details or tricks of the light might appear without his say so, revealing who knows what.

I pointed out that the same might be true of the phonograph. Say you had the recording of a person who subsequently died, you may have captured, along with the impressions of the voice itself and the inevitable distortions – crackles and hisses – a ghostly trace of the deceased.

You could have that kind of conversation with Reuss.

15

I was spending more time than ever on Vasilievsky Island – "Kraut heaven" Zoya called it, because beyond the splendid frontages of the stock exchange, the Academy of Sciences, the University and the rostral columns on the Spit was the old German quarter. There was the cemetery, Pöhl's Apotheke, St Catherine's Lutheran Church, where a kiosk sold the *Petersburger Zeitung* and Gruber's Summer Garden and skittle alley, where they did a very passable *Süppchen von gelber Paprika* with a generous helping of buttered croutons. I never took to Gruber or the head pot man, who may have been his son; I always had the feeling they were laughing behind my back.

Gruber on the other hand was fairly easy-going about the time you spent on a drink and didn't give you a funny look if you occasionally opted for Seltzer rather than the house pilsner. You could also read the newspapers for free, and it was in the classifieds that a particular line in a notice caught my eye:

"Frau Reichhart has been tested by no fewer than three corresponding members of the Society for Psychical Research. Testimonials available on request."

I read on: Callers would be admitted on a first-come, first-served basis, after purchasing a subscription ticket (six weekly sessions,

35 rubles). Thirty-five rubles, to keep the hoi-poloi at bay, I supposed. But it wouldn't be me who was paying and it might be the last chance to call up Kolya's spirit before it disappeared into the ether for ever.

16

Asking Zoya to attend a séance would have been like asking a Buddhist to carve the Sunday joint. Spiritualism disagreed with her, as did God, religion, the life hereafter and any other dish foreign to her materialist diet. She was allergic to churches of all kinds and had already refused to show me the Kazan Cathedral, nor could I persuade here to so much as climb the dome of St Isaac's because the money from the tickets was used to cover the cost of maintaining the building.

So when we turned on to the Catherine Embankment and came face-to-face with the Church "On Spilled Blood", I knew to tread carefully.

'Isn't that where Tsar Alexander was assassinated? It reminds me a bit of St Basil's.'

'Tourist. Is that what it says in Baedecker?'

I was a bloody tourist. I told her to wait; I was going to take a closer look.

We were on the way to the bank to withdraw her first month's salary, so I could be sure she would stick around.

Lavish was the only way to describe the interior which was as tasteless to my way of thinking as the lobby of the Odessa

Metropol. I spent a small fortune on a brochure in German with colour reproductions, then joined the queue for the shrine to the martyred emperor. When my turn came, I dutifully nodded in the direction of the framed icon before peering over the rail at the original pavement where, according to the brochure, you could still see bloodstains.

Coming out I spotted Zoya by the bridge, her back to the canal, resting her elbows against the railing in a most unladylike slouch and with the express intention, it seemed to me of getting a rise out of the *gorodovoi* who happened to be passing at the time. Or was it the pose of a militant atheist giving the finger to the credulous masses?

'So, did you kiss the icon?'

'The Church "On Spilled Blood" is covered with 7,500 square metres of Carrara marble and an equal amount of mosaics (more than any in the world). On the bell tower there are the coats of arms of 144 Russian provinces cities and towns. The Holy Gates...'

'An obscene waste of money. Think how many schools, hospitals...'

'...Orphanages, I get you. It says here a lot of it came from the donations of ordinary people – I didn't hear you complaining about the flowers for Pushkin's grave. It was worth it though, to see the bloodstains.'

'Ha! The embankment is a public right of way you idiot. Do you really think they would allow people to walk over it without scrubbing the stones first? They got rid of the blood with the debris. It is only the moronic masses who believe the official version.'

"Moronic". I hoped she was having me on.

17

The séances were held in the home of a Frau Strauss. I was first to arrive and volunteered to lend a hand with the setting up. One of the servants looked to the seating, while I drew the curtains, lit the red lamp, removed the cloth from the circular table, laid out writing materials and a glass of water for the medium and generally made myself useful. There was no spirit cabinet but Frau Strauss was very particular about photographs, each of which was assigned to a strategic point in the room (I never did get to the bottom of this).

She asked me who I was trying to reach. Was it a loved one? How long since he passed on?

We were lucky to have Clara Reichart she explained. She came with impeccable credentials and was in great demand back home, appearing in hotels, theatres, libraries, even on one occasion in a railway station waiting room, but rarely at small gatherings.

Frau Reichart turned out to be small, thin and pigeon-breasted, with prominent front teeth and arresting auburn hair which fell over one eye, giving her a sly look I found quite seductive. The black shawl she draped around her shoulders made me think of fortune tellers. Her reputation rested largely on her "control", a Prussian private called Feldman who had been killed at the siege of Magdeburg during the Thirty Years War and whose personality (and voice) she assumed during trance.

On this occasion, Feldman took exception to us for reasons he chose to keep to himself, and his behaviour towards Frau Reichart was un-chivalrous to say the least – he even swore at her on one occasion, a terrible soldierly oath. She refused to be goaded except to screw up her eyes and shake her head violently.

When the session broke up prematurely, we disappointed punters made a dive for the spread prepared for us in the parlour. That was when I got talking to a garrulous old lady with a mottled complexion and wobbling chin who I will call "Madame Blancmange".

Madame B suffered from varicose veins and hobbled about slowly, very slowly and only with the aid of a stick, customized with a rubber tip. I found her an armchair and settled her down so we could talk.

I discovered from her that Clara Reichart had started out as a Munich hairdresser, until, after falling down the cellar stairs and breaking open her head, she began seeing visions. She put Feldman's behaviour down to there being an 'infidel' among us.

Madam B was a psychic herself (now retired) who also claimed some success with reading palms. Like many spiritualists she was enthused by my disability, believing that I might have, unbeknown to me, received special powers as a kind of compensation. I told her the old family story about my aunt seeing me talking to the stone angels in the local cemetery and she seemed genuinely impressed.

When I explained why I was there and the circumstances of Kola's death, she suggested I see a medium specialising in "troubled deaths".

'A school friend you say?'

'Lyon, Institut des Sourds.'

'Not being family yourself makes it harder of course. If there was a relative you could bring with you... But I suppose that's out of the question.'

'There's his mother... and a guardian, Modest Tchaikovsky, but he's in Italy.' I anticipated what she was about to say and tried to put her right. 'Not the composer, his brother.'

She rapped me on the arm with her fan. 'I know exactly who you are referring to. Tchaikovsky's wife is a cousin of mine.' She meant the composer.

'I never knew he was married,' I said, mentally turning the pages of *The Life* for a reference I had missed.

'Oh yes. I can introduce you if you like. Not that you'll get a great deal of sense out of her. And it will have to be during visiting hours.'

'Visiting hours – as in a hospital?'

'It is a hospital of sorts I suppose. No, I mean where they lock up the loonies.' She fanned her quivering chin while I took this in. 'Married to a man twice her age, one of her professors. We were all surprised because she hadn't had many gentlemen friends and as he'd been a bachelor for so long... Then he goes and wriggles out of it, what do you make of that?'

What was I to make of it? There had been a church wedding, in front of witnesses. They had waved them off from the station.

'Next thing we know it wasn't at all what he wanted. There was another woman with a fortune. Already married mind.'

'So what happened?'

'A good question, and one Tanya's been asking herself ever since I shouldn't wonder. She wasn't deranged I can tell you that much. Peculiar I grant you. After the honeymoon her bridegroom refused to see her if you please. The next thing we heard, the brothers had had her committed.'

18

The handwriting was unlike anything I'd ever seen before. It might have been a child's hand in the way the letters were formed – painstakingly in a conscientious effort to please. But what really stood out were the flourishes on the capitals, I was reminded of the grace notes on a piece of music, or maybe the clefs on a stave – I recall having seen something similar on a manuscript of Tchaikovsky's in Klin. Except that the pen used here was completely unsuited to twirls, the nib being too thick, the ink too sooty.

Meeting in the Astoria was going to be awkward since I was no longer welcome there after kicking up the rumpus outside Zoya's door. I would have to stick to the public areas and even there I had the feeling I was being monitored – by Antonov, the under-manager, the flunkeys in their braided jackets and silk stockings, the bellboys, the lift attendants, even, it seemed to me in my worst moments, the couriers.

On arrival, I found the nearest full-length mirror and straightened my tie. I was recalling what Zoya had said about signing the visitor's book at Klin with my real name. They were sure to look, if only out of curiosity.

Sofronov was alone, sitting a little adrift from the table, one arm thrown casually over the back of a chair, legs crossed, right foot wagging rhythmically to the music. I had no trouble recognising him because he was the only man in the room not wearing evening dress but a brown-and-yellow-checked suit with a flower in the buttonhole and matching two-tone shoes. I would have known him anyway from the photograph – the Tatar cast of his eyes and the way he wore his hair, parted in the middle and with the glossy sheen you get from applying pomade.

I don't remember a greeting or a handshake, only getting my foot caught in the silk sash which hung like a bridal train from the back of every chair. Out of the corner of my eye, I registered Antonov making his way to the bandstand.

Sofronov waited for the music to finish before drawing closer to the table to eat, gesturing at the assorted *zakuski*: smoked sturgeon, pickled herring, black caviar, marinated cucumbers – though no *bliny* which was a disappointment. The dishes were set out like a flower arrangement, or one of those Dutch Still-Lifes Hoffmann was so fond of where you could, as he said, see your reflection in the gleam of an apple.

19

'Absolut,' said Sofronov pointing to the label. The Astoria was the only hotel in Russia where you could get Swedish vodka. Following his example, I added lemonade to the frosted tumbler which made it taste marginally more palatable, although I would have preferred a beer.

'Can you run to this?' I asked, glancing up at the Winter Garden's spectacular stained glass ceiling, while recalling that even Zoya had baulked at the prices.

It was nothing he hadn't seen before – with Pyotr Ilych they always travelled in style. He knew about the hot running water in every room and that bathrobes were supplied free of charge.

His French was accented but easy to follow since he had shaved off his moustache.

'What's all this about?' (I thought it best to get straight to the point.)

'Enjoy your food. Go on, help yourself. How much was Konradi worth, give or take?'

What kind of a question was that? To buy time I helped myself to the herring.

'I don't get it. What was wrong with saying you were his business manager? You didn't really think we'd be taken in by that cock-and-bull story about Breitkopf and Härtl. Smoke?' he added, proffering a silver case.

I took one before I realised what I was doing and flinched when the flame jetted from the mechanical lighter.

'Come on Brand, how much he was worth? You must have some idea.'

I mimicked the gestures of a smoker while trying to think on my feet. Hoffmann had mentioned a Big Bucks American who had left a fortune – Rockefeller was it, or Carnegie? Was it a million, two million? Still stalling for time, I counted off the villa in Charlottenburg, a property in Florence Hoffman had mentioned, Grankino of course....

'The vineyard in the Caucasus. Yes I know, but how much?'

'Half a million, give or take.'

'Rubles? Dollars?'

I guessed dollars, rightly it would seem because he left it at that and, resting his cigarette in a dip on the edge of the ashtray, helped himself to more fish roe which I watched him spread evenly onto a buttered crust.

'Pyotr Ilych never had dealings with Breitkopf and Härtl,

Jurgenson's were his publishers.'

'Unless you're a spiritualist, it's hard to explain. I was looking for an aura. An aura is like an imprint, the negative on a photograph.' Only then thinking to add that Kolya always spoke fondly of the place. 'These things can be sensed if you know what I mean – usually by a clairvoyant.'

He found this amusing and made no secret of the fact, mocking me with an "Is anybody there?" gesture.

'I told you, you had to be a believer.' As a plausible reason for being in Klin, it was the purest drivel but it was too late to turn back. 'It's true that auras as a rule linger closer to home, around parents – mothers especially.'

'Is that the truth? No chance for me then – I *killed* my mother...'

Did heads turn?

'Not that I had much say in the matter. She died giving birth. Where I come from they call that a "bad death", so I wear this.' He unbuttoned his shirt sufficiently to reveal a silver amulet. 'Leave it off and I'm done for.'

Hoping Antonov had not seen, I lowered my eyes and contemplated the ash accumulating on the edge of my saucer, while trying to figure out where the conversation might be heading.

He called for shot glasses. We were to toast Tchaikovsky who had been dead 20 years come November.

This, he explained, was why we were there. Konradi had promised them various odds and ends – and letters... 'Strictly for the archive.' He would send me a list.

'A travelling show is what I have in mind. Some people turn up their noses.' He raised his glass, 'Their loss. The Maestro's music is more popular than ever – organ grinders play his tunes.'

What he "had in mind" seemed to involve carting memorabilia from Klin to be exhibited at concerts. Visitors would see actual manuscripts and letters; between performances Tchaikovsky's music would be heard on the gramophone where possible.

'Top-notch orchestras, home-in on the tear-jerkers – the dying swan, the death of Hermann, the slow bit from the *Pathetique*.' It was like watching T. J. Barnum introducing Buffalo Bill. He was turning into a showman before my eyes.

Though increasingly woozy, I was enjoying his performance. I was also dimly aware that these ideas were probably not his own, recalling what de Kuyper had told me about Kolya's plans for the travelling exhibition at Grankino.

'A pity Maestro died too early for the cinema.'

There had been a cine camera at Astapavo, he explained, filming Tolstoy on his deathbed; the world's press had tracked him down. I had to admit that from a commercial point of view it would have been a shrewd move.

'Modest Ilych begs to differ, but there are so many anniversaries this year – our emperor, your emperor – and we must see that Maestro gets his due.'

He took a piece of paper and a fountain pen from his inside pocket and began writing – only the one word but his tongue showed with the effort. 'Maidanovo, not Klin. Konradi came to see us at Maidanovo. But never mind that now. We need to talk about Modest Ilych. It is Modest Ilych you're really interested in. Kot suspected as much. He is very observant.'

'You'd be surprised how many people think that. It nearly got me thrown out of the Caffè Greco. They took me for a journalist.'

' "They" being?'

'Just friends of his. You're right though I did want to talk to him as it happens.'

'There you see.'

'We're trying to tie up a few loose ends relating to Kolya's death.

The family think there may have been foul play.'

'Open and shut case. What's to investigate?'

'The problem has been getting access to Modest Ilych. Your man at the embassy, Persiani, thought he'd pulled off a coup, bringing the two of them together. Tchaikovsky could turn out to be a valuable witness. But until we hear what he has to say there's no way of knowing.'

'You're talking in riddles Brand. I don't see why they're wasting so much time on him. You and I know he was a hard-nosed bastard – or maybe that's a side of him you didn't see. After all we did for him.'

'We?'

'Buried his head in Maestro's lap, sobbing his heart out like a kid, "What am I going to do? You tell him, uncle. I can't bear it a moment longer." *What* he couldn't bear was us wanting our fair share.'

Sofronov poured himself another shot. 'Swedish,' he explained for the second time.

'Fair share of what? You can't mean his inheritance?'

'You don't know the half of it. All he was waiting for was his freedom. Within a week of his 21st birthday he had pulled out of the lease on the flat in St Petersburg and left us high and dry.'

He patted his pockets for his lighter. I pointed to the table.

'He was fond of me too you know, Pyotr Ilych.'

He was jealous. No wonder Sofronov bore Kolya a grudge.

Here he was again, standing on his rights, 'That's one thing I learnt from Konradi: take care of number one. Do you think I would let them turn me out of my own home twice? No fear. No-one gets the better of Alyosha Sofronov in matters of business. Well, when I bought Klin that showed them. Pyotr Ilych understood. Why else do you think left me the furniture?'

'You *own* Klin?'

'Why not? It was me who negotiated the lease. When it came on the market, I was ready with the deposit. I may be a servant, but I am a better risk than Modest Ilych.'

The napkin was chafing my neck. I removed it and spread it out on the tablecloth in front of me. 'You said you wanted me to hand over letters. You'll have to be a bit more specific.'

I hoped he would take the bait and ask me directly about the letter Kolya had referred to in the Blue Book. But he shied away.

When I next looked up, a change had come over him. There was more to it than the drink. It was as if he were rehearsing a role in a play. His gestures were becoming more effusive, his delivery almost studied. Perhaps he was imagining himself a character in one of Modest Ilych's – melodramas were they?

'Memories were all he had left. *'The Queen of Spades*, now, I remember Maestro setting Hermann's last words to music as if it were yesterday. When I told him it was time to finish, he was too involved in his work to pay attention. "Just ten more minutes, Lyolya," he said, taking out his watch. It was more like an hour and when he came in for lunch there were tears rolling down his cheeks. And this is what he said – to me, Alyosha: "My opera is finished Lyolya and when you hear it in the theatre, when Hermann dies at the end, you too will be moved to tears." I did cry too, I'm not ashamed to say.'

He took out a handkerchief and wiped his eyes, and then he smiled the way a girl does when she is slightly ashamed of her emotions getting the better of her.

People at the neighbouring table were starting to notice; Antonov too was eying us keenly.

Sofronov struggled to his feet and leaned on the table for support before lurching to the door.

20

"Salvarsan: the drug that saves lives, now on prescription from Hoechst." What is it about the looping copperplate slogan in the window of Waldmann's chemists that sets my heart pounding? I don't have VD, I've been clean altogether for at least a year and anyway, isn't the discovery of a "magic bullet" good news all round? I hear an echo in my head, words spoken. I am back in the doctor's clinic in St Petersburg....

Jewish name, sixtyish, yellow teeth, a chain smoker from the school that exhales with the cigarette still glued to the lips, so that with every outward breath, crumbs of ash break off from the smouldering embers. He had finished probing my balls with his icy fingers, when I threw in casually that I'd seen something about a new treatment. There was another name for Salvarsan, Latin-sounding, I had always been meaning to write down.

Odd that I should remember that particular visit. It often seems to me that digging out a memory from the darker recesses of the brain is a bit like searching for a book in the public library. In the brain (or is it the mind?) there must be something acting as a librarian that knows the cataloguing system inside out, knows which filing cabinet holds the index card for the required memory.

The index card, like the advert in the shop window, is a kind of prompt which may conceivably contain more information for the brain than first meets the eye. Were there other prods to the memory, lurking in the sign which drew my attention before I was even aware of it? And what about when the card is in the right place, but the item itself – the book – has disappeared from the shelves, or been misplaced. Take the word on the shopping list I was unable to read and had forgotten – Kohlrabi. It was only when I kicked the cabbage out of the road to amuse Strammer Max, that my memory was given a nudge in the right direction.

In my lunch hour I worry about Josef. Unless business picks up in the next few months, I see no alternative to letting him go. But go where? What will he live on? Who will support him? He mentioned a relative in the Ruhr, a brother?

I should have seen it coming. How could a small business like mine compete with a department store selling cycles on the instalment plan? I had the same uneasy feeling when I discovered that entrepreneurs like Kolya were ordering from catalogues. Now the war has made life even more complicated and if the fighting is not over by the end of the year, the bottom may have dropped out of the market altogether. Touting for custom at the Empress Augusta Barracks – Krause's idea – sounded promising but got me nowhere. The army is training its own mechanics, I was told. Diversify is what I may have to do – stock cigarettes, sweets, toys even. Perhaps if I were to persuade Josef to go out with a sandwich board...

Trieste is in the newspapers again: "Rioters take to the street. Scuffles with police. Shop windows broken." Italy is on the point of changing sides it would seem. On the inside page, I find a single column about a rumoured military call-up and indignant women marching on the Town Hall. Their placards demand: "Leave our men where they're needed – at home".

The Home Front, where it's still business as usual in the cinemas and music halls I notice. Good for morale, I suppose, so why the iron grill barring the door to the billiard hall? Where's the logic in that? I see someone has now added a sarcastic comment to the notice closing the place down by order: "See you on victory day!" Taking a bit of a chance I'd say, defacing a public announcement must be an offence. All the same I agree with the sentiment.

Do all the Great Powers have it in for billiard halls, I wonder. Is it the same story in St Petersburg? What was that lad's name in Dobrynina's, the Englishman? He had a knack with the stance – he would lean right over the table, using the cue as a line of sight.

Another echo; my own voice this time, "Damn it not in the middle of a break". I must have been on a winning streak when the note from Zoya arrived via the commissionaire. She always knew where to find me it seemed.

21

There was someone I had to meet, an actor at the Aleksandrovsky Theatre who had known the Tchaikovskys. She had "just happened" to be leafing through the back numbers of *The New Times* in the reading room of the Imperial Library.

Really? I suspected her source was someone she had met at Alina's, but kept my thoughts to myself.

When we met in the Summer Gardens, I tucked Baedecker under one arm in a clumsy attempt to keep her from seeing it but, instead of mocking me, she asked where I was going.

'Actually, Peterhof.'
'If you can wait till Saturday, there's an excursion by boat that leaves from the pier near the Hermitage. We can go together.'

I pictured us enjoying a packed lunch from Yeliseev's in the palace grounds, then a snooze or a stroll through the park. I would buy her an ice and we would sit on a bench overlooking the Gulf and watch the sun go down, like Gurov and the lady with the lapdog in that place in the Crimea. She would be wearing her pale blue dress and carrying a sun umbrella and we would walk arm in arm, just like old times...

Saturday came. People were boarding and there was still no sign of her. I stood to the side of the gangplank to let a deckhand wave on a party of cyclists. Already the ship's engines were throbbing while the water churned below.

After the steamer had left and the wash was reduced to lapping the bottommost steps, I noticed that the quayside was scattered with rose petals from a party or wedding – a champagne bottle with a broken neck, glinted green in the sunlight.

That was when I first wondered if she wanted me out of the way.

22

Did she really think I would go on without her? Or was she expecting me to shrug my shoulders and go home without bothering to check at the hotel, at *Wiener Chic,* the hairdressers, the jewellers in the shopping arcade, Bulla's the photographers?

She not alone in Dominique's and had chosen our booth with the view of the cathedral colonnade. She was as ravishing as ever. It would have been easier on me if I had detected even the smallest blemish – a smudge of make-up, a few loose hairs.

I closed the distance between us until I could follow the rapid ebb and flow of her breathing beneath the pleated silk of her blouse. Yet so intent was she on holding the attention of this stranger – he raised a hand in a calming gesture that only made her more insistent – so bent on making her point that she failed to notice me. She was *'Tellement fatigue de cette...' canard*? (I was listening in with my eyes, "Deaf people make good spies", had she said that?) No, *charade...* before a name beginning with a plosive, but with two syllables, so not Brand.

I watched her draw out a white envelope from a beaded bag with gold thread identical to one she had pointed out to me in the window of Merten's.

It was like the climatic scene of a film when you are so caught up in what is happening on the screen, that for an instance you become totally oblivious to your surroundings.

What was I doing there? Did I want to have it out with her? Even at that late moment it might have been possible for me to turn my back on them and slip away. Then why did I feel compelled to step forward and assume the role assigned to me in this drama of her devising?

Her momentary loss of composure had been enough to alert the stranger who slid from his seat, without showing his face, and disappeared.

'Satisfied now?' she said, calling for the bill.

It was while she was distracted that I noticed the envelope lying on a sunlit patch of carpet. I recovered it with the toe of my shoe and transferred it smartly to the inside pocket of my jacket.

23

I have no memory of leaving Dominique's but somehow or other I found myself on the Fontanka. Not strictly true – I do remember trying to cross the Anichkov Bridge because I was nearly run over by a tram. Everyone else looked happy on that warm summer's afternoon while I, imagining myself to be Goethe's hero in *Young Werther* was "waiting on the morning in tears." I walked quickly, purposely, eyes fixed on some point in the distance, as if I was late for an urgent appointment whereas in fact I had no goal in mind except to walk and keep on walking. At the same time I was not aware of any sense of progression, of going forward; it felt like I was walking on the spot, or treading water; that's it, I was like a sleepwalker treading water. The humidity may have had something to do with it. The day had turned sultry. The sun still shone from time to time but dully, the light filtering through clouds that were turning a sickly yellow. The strange thing was that, despite everything she had put me through and with, realistically, zero expectations of anything positive coming out of the experience, there remained a small part of me that hoped she might be following on behind. Was that why I stopped at the bridge, to give her time to catch up, to lay a comforting hand on my shoulder; and then, when I continued to stare resolutely down into the water, to turn me around so that she could apologise for the wrong she had done me, beg for forgiveness, demand to be given a second chance? Then I had what I can only describe as a momentary blackout. All I can recall I was setting my jaw, clenching my fists and tensing every muscle in my upper body, as if there was a huge weight I was straining to lift but which would likely be beyond me. I was making so much effort that I had forgotten to breathe. And then a hysterical thought came out of nowhere, a kind of vision I suppose you might call it. I was at my workbench and had Zoya's head clamped into the vice. I was turning the handle by degrees, waiting for something to happen. I imagined that at some point, when the pressure on the temples became too much there would be a creaking sound. Her skin would turn blue or maybe purple, there would be contusions, blood would seep from her mouth, her eyes would bulge, bones would begin to crack and splinter. At that moment it occurred to me that this frenzied, sadistic cruelty must be akin to what a murderer feels when, no longer capable of keeping his feelings in check, he has no alternative but to act.

Then I broke down. In three days it would be her birthday. I had already decided on a present, a bag, and had even gone as far as ordering it from Duce's. I must have been crying because a passer-by stopped to ask me if I was alright but, full of shame, I waived him away. I hurried on, past a church with a deep blue dome and gold stars painted on, government offices that seemed to stretch in front of me like a rubber band, over the bridge with the sphinxes, then on until the theatre too was behind me, not stopping until I got to a dockyard which was patrolled by sentries in naval uniform. I turned around before they had a chance to ask me what I was doing there.

Around me everyone was running for cover. They must have thought it strange that buffeted by gusts and squalls of pelting rain, I alone seemed in no particular hurry, that I too wasn't rushing to shelter in a crowded doorway, or at least covering my head with a jacket or newspaper – an umbrella would have been no use and in the confusion of picking up Zoya's letter I had left my hat behind in Domenique's.

One memory that comes back to me is brooding about Gerda and Reuss on the way to the Pension. I suppose it was the odours rising from the river – oil spills from lighters and barge tugs, chemicals, effluent, the stench of the Landwehr Canal as you cross the Luisen Ufer. 'Thank you for being so understanding, dearest Theo' (she had written). 'You have no idea how happy you are making me.' Understand? I did not understand at all!

24

In the Apraksin Market I bought a half bottle of brandy from a wine merchant's — proper cognac, not the Armenian muck they have a mind to palm you off with. Ma Ritter being teetotal herself and pro-temperance, booze was banned from the premises, so I slipped into the back courtyard through the archway and took the kitchen stairs, which led eventually to my room and the fire escape. I had put the aching in my joints down to the exertions of the walk. Now though, as I began to shiver uncontrollably I realised that I was succumbing to something.

I couldn't decide whether to get out of my wet clothes first or break open the brandy. I compromised, stripping down to my underwear before unscrewing the cap on the bottle and swallowing a good three fingers' worth. Then I fetched a towel from the bathroom across the corridor and dried my hair. I was soaked through as rainwater had seeped through the silk lining of my jacket. Being as careful as I could, I extricated the loose bank notes from my pockets and smoothed them out on the table. My fingers were rigid with cold, so that the simple act of striking a match caused me no end of difficulty. Then, as I was attempting to twist the candle into the holder I was scalded with dripping wax. I dried out the bills, starting with the 25 roubles, then unpeeled the letter from the envelope and held it over the flame.

"Dear Estelle...the costumes worn at *Thés Dansants* this season...keeping my eyes open...the three-flounce skirt is coming in again... straight and straighter is this season's motto..."

It was the kind of thing I used to come across thumbing through the pages of *Vanity Fair* or the *Journal des Demoiselles* while I waited for her to finish work at Tiriocchi's. Why hadn't I confronted her in Domenique's, probed for inconsistencies in her story, evasions, falsehoods? I was left feeling cheated, outflanked. If it had been a business meeting why had Sonny Boy been in so much of a hurry to get out of my way? Obviously they were having an affair but there was nothing in the way of evidence here. The possibility occurred to me that the cunning little bitch might still find a way to wriggle out of it, like Houdini escaping from the Water Torture Cell.

There is a certain class of film, a "suspense story" they call it on the billing, which turns on the moment when things start to become clear. A struggling artist, say, invites a woman to have her portrait painted. We know from the off what game he is playing, but it is only when the girl is undressing for him behind the screen and you can see him fingering the open blade of a pair of dressmaker's scissors, that you realise what his real intentions are.

I had noticed a change in the colouration of the paper, just below the line beginning "black and white are extremely popular."

Another message was appearing, faint but clearly legible:

"Inspector Worther going nowhere with his investigations. Am returning home. Inform Barkov"

Barkov – the plosive with two syllables.

In the same instant something else occurred to me, something that had been troubling me all along, like an itch that is impossible to locate. It was the explanation she gave for her dismissal from Tirriochi's. Obviously a lie – not because the details were unconvincing; no, she had gone over them again and again so that when she was asked, as she knew she would be, her account would be flawless. It was a lie because there no way the real Zoya would have got herself into that situation. She had too much to lose.

The Lady with the lapdog! At least she had a certain class. I shoved Zoya into a routine I had seen in a nightclub. Made her skinny, but dolled up as if she was on the game. Introduced a couple of workmen in leather waistcoats and aprons, ordered them to strip her without finesse. Then watched them tie her to the cross beams of a whipping post before kicking her legs into a splayed position (a nice touch) and setting about her with their belts. Suffer bitch. Flinch. Shudder. In this admittedly sick fantasy I alone had the power to put a stop to her humiliation but looked on with indifference.

Until a more pressing, a more urgent reality intervened to bring me down to earth: if Gerda married, I would be on my own.

I touched my forehead and realised that I was running a temperature. The brandy was losing its effect. My head ached and there was a terrible dryness in my mouth as if my tongue was glued to my palate. I opened the cupboard where I kept a supply of lemonade to compensate for the lack of drinking water and quenched my thirst, before rummaging in my things for the one warm item of clothing I had – the sailor's jumper with the roll neck I had brought with me from Trieste.

I crawled into bed and pulled the cotton coverlet up around my chin. It felt like being a child again, lying with my hands clasped tight and my knees drawn up to my chest.

Mother would have warmed the bed with a water bottle, helped me with the buttons on my shirt, made me a drink of hot milk.

On the night table was a Chinese vase – Pop had picked up a job lot of similar "willow pattern" porcelain while working in Hamburg and there were pieces, some decorative, some functional all over our home in Berlin. My mother was delighted with it, pointing out to visitors the Delft watermark as proof that it was the genuine article.

I reached out from under the covers and touched it with the tips of my fingers. There were hairline cracks on the creamy surface, like capillaries coursing under skin. I found the simplicity of the images: a man fishing, a teahouse, birds in flight, soothing and, closed my eyes a second or third time...

A woman beckons from the blue humpbacked bridge. I follow but she hurries off and, try as I might to catch up, she is always a few paces ahead. I walk with my eyes on her shoulders and her swept up black hair. Then she turns and pauses. I reach out but my fingers get tangled in the silk folds of her robe and she is gone, floating high over the lake before taking flight. I lose sight of her when I am dazzled by light coming in from a window.

Frau Ritter is moving around in the room. Has she has come to empty the chamber pot? I become distraught and start apologising – for the state of the room, for coming in after "lights out", for not stopping to play cards with her other guests, for all the trouble. But who is it pressing a cold flannel to my forehead, tousling my hair? 'Shush.'

Dust motes are settling on a trunk, I see pasted labels, the inside of a baggage hall.

'What's this, dirty pictures?' Zoya hands the photographs to the customs officer who points to an item in the regulations posted on the wall with a white-gloved finger. There are gasps of astonishment from the gallery as two postmen seize me under the arms and drag me off to another hall where tasselled flags protrude like battle trophies from green walls. I join the queue of peasants dressed in smocks and worn felt boots and we shuffle towards the portrait of the Tsar. We submit, bowing and with bound hands...

Like Odysseus in Alina's painting, I was to reflect later, I had been beguiled by a beautiful woman and distracted for a while before continuing on my journey and seeing my mission through to the end.

25

Around that time I would go to the window to open the curtains (rarely at the same hour) and down below, but on the opposite side of the street, I would see a man, fairly nondescript, standing at the corner. At first I assumed he was meeting someone and thought no more about it but one day, after staying put at the window for maybe five minutes, I caught him glancing up at me. Then there was the day I was cycling to Vasilevsky Island and was aware of being tailed by a cyclist riding behind me, following more or less the same route but at a discreet distance. The clincher was late one night when returning home after a skinful and needing to change trams from the no.4 to the no.6, I was aware of another passenger doing the same. Coincidence? So I thought until getting off the no. 6 at Italianskaya, I turned around to see him alight from the rear car.

Strangely these accumulated experiences did not unnerve me; if anything they had the opposite effect. I reasoned that if Barkov had gone to so much trouble to recruit Zoya and persuade her to follow me all the way to Russia, then if he was having me tailed, I must be on to *something*.

I was still digesting the information Zoya had given me about Modest Ilych somehow being responsible for Tchaikovsky's death. According to her, no one in their right mind drank unboiled tap water in St Petersburg – I myself had seen warning signs to that effect. The newspapers had seized on the implication that Modest Ilych had been slow to fetch a doctor and his decision to go ahead with the premier of his play, aroused even greater controversy.

The only way to make sense of any of it was to follow up on Zoya's, or was it Alina's invitation to meet the actor Konstantin Varlamov.

I notice the signed photograph, standing on the mantelpiece, needs a dusting.

Gerda looked him up: In a distinguished career spanning more than 30 years, this comic genius... best remembered for... "meritorious artist of the Imperial Theatres".

Léon on the other hand will never be famous and I have nothing to remember him by. Yet *his* features are clear in my mind, while Varlamov's, were it not for the photograph would be no more than a blur. Why is that, I wonder? Is it the makeup getting in the way? Without this mask his face was, I was surprised to discover, utterly unmemorable.

When I arrived that evening, Varlamov was dressed in the style of a French aristo with powdered wig, brocaded waistcoat and buckled shoes. I followed him into his dressing room and waited while he sank into the chair in front of the illuminated mirror and, cupping his chin in the palms of his hands, his elbows propped up on the table, stared moodily at his reflection for what seemed an awfully long time.

I found a stool and took in my surroundings. On the dressing table were make-up sticks and moisturising cream, a dirty cup, a slouching china doll with a lazy eye. Reflected in the mirror was a calendar and, pinned to a bulletin board on the wall, the good luck telegrams from well-wishers. I also recall a smell of disinfectant, powerful enough to cut through the scent from the floral bouquet Varlamov had dumped unceremoniously on the floor.

I turned to see a sharp-eyed little man prop open the swing door with his foot while carrying in a steaming basin of water. Léon, Varlamov's dresser, was wearing black from head to toe like an actor from another play, another period – Hamlet? I thought I must be sitting on his stool because on noticing me he shrugged his shoulders in silent protest. But it was just his manner – like a hairdresser he seemed used to being on his feet.

As if touched by a magician's wand, Varlamov sprang to life. 'He owns a bicycle shop Leon, in Berlin. Imagine!'

He spoke about it as if I was a trapeze artist or a walker on the high wire.

'He rides here, in Petersburg. Did you hear that Leon, to the islands. Extraordinary! I shall come to you for lessons, see if I don't.'

I tried to explain the reason for my being there, but, as if they had been waiting outside for a signal, a stream of visitors now poured in: delivery boys, members of the public hoping for an autograph, fellow actors, friends, just wanting to say hello, offer their congratulations, drop off flowers or boxes of chocolates... Corks popped and the champagne (Crimean Sekt) flowed. Well, I was in no hurry, what I had to say could wait for Léon to help Konstantin Vasilievich out of his coat, top up his glass, hand him a towel, a cotton ball or the little solution of make-up remover. Leon's hair too was greying but his quick, nimble movements that made me think of fencing and rapiers. Hamlet again?

Eventually the room cleared except for the matinee idol – dark mysterious eyes that were constantly on the move and did most of his talking for him, hair curled and sculpted like a Roman emperor's and a soft almost feminine jaw. This was the famous tenor, Leonid Sobinov, who had sung at La Scala and was on first name terms with Chaliapin (a trophy for Gerda's autograph book). Coming in he did an extraordinary thing: purporting to spot a loose thread on the cuff of Varlamov's embroidered jacket he made great play of snapping it off, twirling it around his head several times, then tucking it into his pocket; at which point they all cried out: "to the devil!"

Konradi. The problem, I had to understand was Pyotr Ilych's generous nature. There were so many young men he had given a helping hand to over the years, aspiring artists and musicians, promising talents whose careers he had promoted or supported in other ways. Various candidates were touted, potential matches identified, then rejected like socks tossed from a drawer and discarded. One played the mandolin, or guitar. Another was a remarkable mimic and member of a 'set' with a musical nickname no one could recall. Leon, who was surely too young to help, made his own suggestions nevertheless.

I was sensing a nostalgic turn in the conversation which would lead nowhere, when Sobinov sprang to his feet, thrust out his arms to make wings and kicked his right leg into the air, 'I have him. He means the chorus girl!'

'And the walk,' Varlamov said. 'Do the walk, Leonid Vitalyevich, you remember.'

Sobinov closed his eyes for a moment as if gathering his thoughts. Then, glancing at the mirror to make sure he had Varlamov's attention took a turn across the room, sticking out his bottom and wiggling his hips suggestively.

This was too much. It was nothing like Kolya, but Sobinov's tale rolled on.

'Then someone, a relative, put his foot down.'

'*Her* foot down,' Varlamov countered. 'She was a Countess somebody or other. She feared a scandal and the poor boy simply vanished overnight...'

'To be shoe-horned into the Preobrazhensky Life Guards. That the fellow you mean – hair oil, carefully waxed moustache, monocle?'

'Pyotr Ilych went to no end of trouble trying to put a stop to it – writing letters, buttonholing ministers, raising it with the... the War Department or whatever they call it.'

'No, no, no – you're confusing him with one of the servants – Alyosha. He was drafted into military service. Tchaikovsky had to buy him out.'

Alyosha had at least mixed in the same circles. I wrote the name down for them again in my notebook. 'Konradi, Kolya Konradi. He was like me, couldn't hear.'

Varlamov turned to Sobinov, 'He means the ward. Excuse me for speaking bluntly about your friend, but that one always struck me as a nonentity. Nothing to do with his deafness you understand, he masked that rather well in fact, all things considered. It was just that... there was nothing remarkable about him, nothing at all.'

'Until the funeral. That was a side of him we hadn't seen.'

'Poor fellow. He was distraught, absolutely inconsolable. They had to drag him away from the coffin, it caused quite a scandal. He actually kissed the corpse. We all feared for his health; after all, the body might have been contagious.'

'We didn't realise how things stood between them until then.'

'Kissed the corpse *on the lips.*'

'Now Kostya...'

The memory triggered a series of reminiscences that suggested to me at least that while Kolya's behaviour may have been unusual, even a touch excessive, it did reflect the popular feeling towards Tchaikovsky at the time.

So many well-wishers had gathered outside the flat during his last illness that a police guard had been posted at the door to stop the crush of people anxious to read the daily bulletin on the state of his health. On the day of the funeral both of them had joined the thousands of mourners who descended on the piazza in front of the Kazan Cathedral to watch the cortege pass.

'It was all so sudden.' Varlamov said. 'Pyotr Ilych had been sitting in this very dressing room, days before he was taken ill.'

Leon was re-sewing a button on Varlamov's costume as deftly as Zoya might have done, though his hands looked too big for the task and his fingers were surprisingly bony.

Varlamov continued with his story. 'That was on the Tuesday. I remember because there was no matinee. He dropped in during the interval and we chatted about... about spiritualism, the tarot.'

'That was nice of him, dropping in like that,' said Leon, musing to himself.

'Oh there was never any side to Pyotr Ilych.'

'After the performance we all went out to Leiner's restaurant. Pyotr Ilych had the macaroni. Odd me remembering a detail like that.'

Over supper they had discussed Modest Ilych's latest play which was then in rehearsal. For no particular reason I jotted down the title: *Prejudices*, while Varlamov went on:

'He was the kindest of men as a rule but when he thought the occasion merited, he could wield his tongue like a scourge. That's so, isn't it Leonid?'

Sobinov looked up from the newspaper to nod an affirmative.

'That night he really took his brother to task. "It hasn't a hope. If you want to be taken seriously why won't you take the necessary pains? I told you: cut, cut, cut – the whole thing is far too long and on top of that, there isn't enough humour, especially in the first act. As it is, your play never rises above mediocrity."

'And was he right' I asked – 'about it "not having a hope"?'

Varlamov said, 'The audience was hardly in the mood. I mean, to premier on the day of your brother's funeral. What *didn't* go wrong? A card table went missing, just as the curtain was about to go up for the second act; Savina fluffed her lines, I left out an entire speech....'

Sobinov put his paper to one side. 'We've been through all this with that journalist.'

'That's right. I have his card somewhere. There was a newspaperman here last week asking questions.'

Varlamov took his wallet from his jacket, unsnapped the ticket pocket and went through his cards until he found the right one.

I turned a page in my notebook and scribbled it down: "Journalist".

Sobinov said, 'That was what was odd about him He didn't carry a notebook. He didn't write a single thing down in fact. He was mainly interested in confirming things he already knew. Not much of a story there.'

'There was one question where you said he was being impertinent.' This came from Leon. 'Remember – when he said about there being people who still believe that Pyotr Ilych took his own life.'

In Italy – Tivoli it must have been, when Hoffmann mentioned a journalist stirring up trouble for Kolya, he may as well have been speaking of the King of Siam. Now I was in Petersburg and this journalist had a name; not only a name – if I'd had a mind, I could have summoned him to the telephone.

I was getting somewhere.

26

I think of him now as two people. There is Alyosha and there is Sofronov.

Alyosha is the boy in the photograph on the mantelpiece in Klin: smirking insolent, full of himself. I see his bowler no longer straight but tilted on the back of his head in a rakish manner, his thumbs stuck in the ticket pockets of his waistcoat. I imagine him flaunting a watch on a gold chain he had wheedled out of his master. I see a 'loosey', slightly moist, dangling from his lips and his face is flushed with drink. It was a type I had come across often enough, perched on a bar stool in the darkest corner of the kneipe, cheeking the barmaid or making suggestive remarks – a pickpocket or a bookie's runner.

Now, how had this boy from the backwoods risen from hired-hand to lord of the manor? By "standing on his rights" – the right, as Sofronov saw it, to make his own way in the world. He is the seasoned burglar breaking into society with a jemmy or lock-pick depending on the degree of resistance; who, after gaining entry, makes himself at home while taking a professional interest, evaluating what is on open display before trying drawers, cupboards, the backs of picture frames. Then, confident that he won't be caught, he indulges his curiosity, leafing through diaries, perusing the odd letter, running a finger over bank statements, shaking a few books to see what falls out. Not looking for anything in particular, just being thorough.

Either of them might have left me with the bill that night in the Winter Garden – for the premium vodka, the outrageously dear hors d'oeuvres, the cover charge, a tax I couldn't fathom but had to pay anyway, the gratuity for the orchestra – a dirty trick that I wouldn't forget in a hurry.

27

When I did run into him again, it was when I least expected.

I was watching a black saloon with a closed top being dredged from the canal by a wooden hoist. I had mingled with the crowd out of curiosity and was trying to make out what they were saying. A freak accident, a collision with a passing cart. The driver of the black saloon had got out to use the starting crank but had forgotten to apply the parking break, leaving the car to roll into the water.

I felt a tugging on my arm and turned to see Sofronov. He wanted to know what was going on so I filled him in as far as I was able. From the other onlookers, he established that there was a woman passenger in the car, a governess – French or English, he wasn't sure which.

'Poor bastard – him with the blanket over his head – the driver. He's for it.'

Now the car was swaying above the embankment, the front passenger door swinging on its hinges. We all moved back to avoid a dowsing.

'Ever seen a drowned body? They clench their fists – like this.'

'Struggling for air I expect. Someone you knew?'

'Same village. Fished out of a river, couldn't swim.'

I was thinking of Kolya kissing Pyotr Ilych's dead body.

'Tell me something: would you kiss a corpse if it had cholera? Kolya did.'

'I'll have to take your word for that. Risky I'd say.'

'But you went to the funeral?'

'Leaving the house they nearly dropped the coffin. Too many people on the stairs. I'll show you his grave if you like. It won't take long.'

He took my shrug as assent and whistled for a cab.

We pulled up outside the gates of the Aleksander Nevsky Monastery where Sofronov bought a small bunch of chrysanthemums. He exchanged a few words with the gatekeeper before leading me briskly into the cemetery. We picked our way through tombstones and monuments until we were almost at the perimeter wall.

Tchaikovsky's marble bust stood on a stone plinth, framed by a pair of mourning angels, one male, one female. When Sofronov removed his hat, I followed suit. He laid the flowers then stood on the edge of the grave, head bowed while taking a furtive look at his watch. I too lowered my head. My mind was still on the death of the governess. How would the chauffeur be feeling? Like the tram driver who had accidentally run into Frieda?

While I was occupied with these thoughts, I was conscious of Sofronov giving me sly sidelong glances. Straightening up, he turned to me and said, 'Well?'

'Well what?'

'Are you getting anything – vibrations, signs of life?'

I couldn't help smiling at this. 'What are you talking about? The man's been dead twenty years.'

He shook his head impatiently. 'You know what I mean. Do whatever it is you do. Use your powers, concentrate. Ask him something.'

'For instance?'

'Ask him did he mean to drink the water.'

'Seriously?'

'Ask him! Ask him about his last letter to Konradi.'

'You're having me on! You can't really believe that getting through to Pyotr Ilych is as easy as ringing him up on the telephone.'

He glared at me, his hands thrust deep into his pockets. He was muttering something but too far away for me to read his lips. When I didn't respond he came close enough for me to smell the garlic on his breath, seized me by the shoulders, then bawled, droplets of spittle landing on my cheeks.

I pushed him away. So I was a fraud, was I? Why so interested in that letter? What's in it, that made it worth going to Rome for? Or maybe I should ask Modest Ilych.'

'Why bring him into this? Anyway you're too late. He won't see you now, Modest Ilych is dying.'

With that, he left me with Pyotr Ilych and the angels.

28

Sofronov's outburst had unnerved me. It was not him I was afraid of, but his connections. He was the kind of man to have "associates", contacts with the criminal underworld. I had no evidence to base this on, it was just a hunch but if I was right, then I was in need of protection. I was like Odysseus in Alina's painting, I had come to expect unpleasant surprises, unseen forces blowing me off-course in unchartered waters, siren voices, quarrelling gods plotting a haphazard course and propelling me towards a fate they had yet to agree on.

I can clearly recall running my finger along the serrated edge of the business card Varlamov had given me:

"T.J.S Stevens. Investigative reporter.

Member of the National Union of Journalists (Great Britain).

Honorary member of the American Press Club."

The way I figured it, talking to Stevens would give me a degree of protection, anyone wishing to do me harm would think twice about it if there was a chance of exposure. Something else occurred to me about journalists: Weren't they bound to protect their sources, like doctors with the Hippocratic oath?

I am over the panic attacks now, the night sweats, the accusing voices: 'Are you like them? Then what does that make you?'

though I still get the weird dream about a woman peering over my shoulder in Post Restante. No-one, I kept telling myself, could possibly connect me with Fanucci's photographs, but I believed it only for as long as it took to re-enact the business of getting rid of them: on the train before the border crossing, half the fragments disappearing through the hole in the toilet floor, an impatient rattle of the door – the guard? – jettisoning the rest out of the window.

Girls as young as I liked Stevens had said. 'Girls who swear on their mother's grave that they are fifteen but are really only twelve.' The way he talked, we might have been punters comparing notes on a penny arcade peep show. The "shoddy goods" were sold on to private collectors for modelling work. 'Gentlemen with depraved tastes. *Dépravé.*' He said it with undisguised relish.

I shuddered at the thought of it. And what if Fanucci's premises were raided, what might they find in the way of evidence – records, accounts, membership lists, names and addresses? If my name came up...?

29

I had been looking for Stevens at reception, when I spotted a charabanc with a canvas top and red chassis, following the curve of the Neva, swerving wildly to avoid the potholes. As I went to meet it, the bus veered off the road and along a side-track to the rear of the factory, a brick pile that loomed above a bend in the river, a penitentiary with smokestacks, factory and fortress in one. Not for the first time, it struck me as an odd place for a *rendez-vous* – and on a Sunday.

The bus had parked beside a wooden hut overlooking a sports field. I watched the men get down, a couple of dozen of them, dressed to varying degrees in white; some wore hooped caps, like racing jockeys. It was only when they began unloading their paraphernalia – bats, balls, sticks and the rest – that I realised they were there to play cricket.

"Steer clear of the press, avoid publicity at any cost". I had gone too far already in defying Hoffman to turn back now. My objective was clear enough: shield Kolya while finding out what Stevens had been up to in Italy. By now I had my story off-pat. I would say that

the family, without the knowledge of the Italian authorities, had employed an undercover policeman to dish out summary justice to the petty criminals responsible for Kolya's death. Identify

Barkov by name, blow his cover, why not? Oh wouldn't I enjoy shining a torch on his burrow, kicking up the dirt. 'That's for using Zoya against me, you bastard.'

Only Stevens wasn't interested in Barkov or the circumstances surrounding Kolya's death. He was an undercover journalist, pandering to the tastes of readers hooked on the lurid and sensational. On sleaze, not to put too fine a point on it. All in a good cause, it goes without saying. He was a crusader wielding the sword of truth and the trusty shield of fair play in the unending battle against corruption and depravity. But shovel away the bullshit and you are left with an almighty stench and a peek at What the Butler Saw.

He couldn't have been serious when he invited me to join him on one of his night prowls, could he? I can still see him blinking up at me through the pebble lenses of his glasses, his bald pate level with my chin. 'To be on the safe side I carry a cosh – keep it hidden of course – for the back alleys around railway stations and public gardens after dark – public conveniences, too before they shut for the night.'

He would introduce himself to the constable patrolling a particular beat and flash his press card – he didn't want him getting the wrong idea. The coppers knew the street girls by name, the regulars. 'You say you are interested in the young ones.'

'Young meaning?'

'As young as you like.'

'As *I* like? Oh no leave me out of it.'

Getting his "Louise" scoop had involved posing as a pimp in Piccadilly Circus. He had procured the girl himself, with the mother's permission, or so he thought. Which was how he ended up doing two years at hard labour. 'The day I came out, there was *The Gazette* waiting to photograph me in my prison garb. I was the story that day – special edition, the full treatment.'

It wouldn't have surprised me if he'd lugged his ball and chain along to the nearest pub and bought everyone a round.

He had it on him, *The Police Gazette of London*. I saw his picture.

We had been sitting on the steps of the clubhouse so that Stevens could keep one eye on the game. I was still trying to make out the caption under the first illustration to his story when he snatched the paper from me and folded it over. 'Start at the end like the rest of my readers,' he said handing it back.

The last illustration showed a room, poorly furnished, with a narrow iron bedstead and a chamber pot. On the little table were the remains of a supper. At the foot of a dirty quilt, the discarded clothes of the girl in the first picture who now lay on top of the bedspread, dressed only in a shift. There were two shadowy figures in the room; one looking on, the other holding what might have been a gag over the girl's mouth and nose. The caption read, "A doctor, struck off for malpractice, attends his 'patient' before the innocent's new 'owner' has his way."

He returned from the clubhouse with two more beers.

'Giving the girl a name plays on their emotions, gets them properly worked up. "If this was your daughter, how would you feel?"'

I pictured these readers of his rushing the courthouse, banging on the roof of the Black Maria. Sitting on the edge of the bed later, hands tucked under my knees, rocking back and forth, I can't get Fanucci's studio out of my head – the girl's chewed finger nails, the dirty soles of her feet, the want of hips.

Left alone with these thoughts was like being lowered by stages in a sealed diving bell, until all you are aware of is the sound of your own breathing. Tethered, the bell is rooted to the spot and left to his own devices the diver can do nothing.

30

He had been nursing a cricket ball in his lap, turning it on the seam when he said, 'Something for nothing, old man: setting about it like that won't get you anywhere in the Greco.'

It was like being on a stepladder and missing my footing after Stevens had given it a tug.

He squinted up at me. 'What put you onto it – or was it a shot in the dark?'

Setting about what? I couldn't get my mind to focus.

' "Denies all knowledge" – duly noted.' He undid his blazer to demonstrate.

Outside was worsted; to see the silk lining, you had to turn it over. The lining was what really went on in the Greco.

'What you stumbled across old son was a calling to order. You spoiled it for them. Meeting adjourned. That's why Pontifex was so cross.'

Pontifex? A meeting of what?

Just then we were interrupted by a teammate telling Stevens to get "padded up".

Was Stevens in the know because he was one of them – a

freemason possibly? I had noticed something unusual about his belt – the clasp. A silver letter S turned on its side, actually a snake. Reuss was fond of this kind of insignia, the stock-in-trade of secret societies.

Stevens was being applauded onto the field; it was his turn to bat. I watched him shape up to the bowler, shoulder thrust forward. He struck the ball firmly and was on his way.

I watched the game without really understanding what was going on. There was an odd ritual every so often when the team on the field changed places and re-formed, a bit like a courtly dance.

I was beginning to lose interest when a cry went up from the middle of the field at which point Stevens turned abruptly, removed his cap and headed back to the clubhouse, shaking his head and replaying the stroke that had got him "out".

When he reappeared, he had a dressing around his thumb which had been struck by the ball and was beginning to swell.

I had still to find out what Stevens was doing in Italy, whether Kolya was on his list of interviewees. Had Stevens too been looking for Modest Ilych in the Caffè Greco? Was it possible he had seen Kolya with Sofronov in Rome? In pursuing this agenda of mine it would be better, I decided, to take a circuitous route, go all round the houses if necessary, show a bit of guile. I appealed to his sense of self-importance. 'As a media man can you think of any reason for Sofronov to worry about the coverage of Tchaikovsky's anniversary?'

'If only poor old Modest Ilych had got his story straight, hadn't got himself into such a muddle over the details – when his brother first complained of feeling unwell. Why the delay in calling the doctor? If cholera was suspected, why not bring in a consultant, a specialist? – When the public takes a great man to their hearts, they want the truth. They feel cheated when they sense things are being brushed under the carpet.'

I wondered if this was the angle he had been working on in Italy.

'The frustrating thing is, it has the prints of the School of Jurisprudence all over it. Every fibre of my journalistic being confirms that to be the case. I am like a bloodhound Brand, trained to the peak of fitness and hot on the scent. They won't out-run me for ever.'

He was referring to the possibility that Tchaikovsky had deliberately drunk contaminated water. There was another possibility – a toxicologist had pointed out at the time that the symptoms of cholera were consistent with those of arsenic poisoning.

'Ask yourself about his state of mind. That gloomy symphony of his, The Tragic.'

I corrected him.

'Pathetique, tragic. What's the difference. Morbid is what it is.'

It was enough for Stevens that the newspapers had been ordered to kill the story. Who gave the order was what Stevens wanted to know. Why the cover-up?

31

I was getting pins and needles and stood up to stretch my legs. 'What were you saying about a school?'

The Imperial School of Jurisprudence.

'Not one so much as breaks into a run. No horseplay. Strange don't you think?' He had been watching the boys coming out of the main gate. 'You would expect a bit of healthy rough and tumble from the younger boys at least.'

In Germany he would have been picked up for voyeurism, possibly charged with "loitering with intent". I assumed he had paid off the duty cop.

I looked up to see the ball scudding towards me until it was intercepted by the deft forearm of the fieldsman standing on the edge of the field.

'You must have come across them – on the Fontanka – they wear green blazers. Green with gold buttons.'

Beside him was a leather satchel. He dug out a pack of record cards held together by a rubber band – his portable office, he explained. The cards, were for the Class of "62". He removed the band to let me take a look.

Most of the alumni went on to become judges, government

ministers, Justices of the Peace. I found one for Tchaikovsky, PI and a poet, somebody Apukhtin. I had also seen the name Konradi, typed like the others at the top left hand corner, next to the punch hole, but the initials belonged to Kolya's father. I asked to see one of the cards again – something had caught my eye, a small detail. Next to Prince Chersky, A D was the single word, Pontifex.

Pontifex – meeting adjourned, the Caffè Greco.

It was Pontifex who put the fear of god into eavesdroppers at the Greco; Pontifex who masqueraded in my dream as a snarling bulldog with gold plated jaws; Pontifex who was the shadowy presence on the hotel balcony at Tivoli; Pontifex who was demonised in our role-plays at Chateau Perache. Almost without realising it I had stumbled on the right connections, the silk lining. Order a sequence correctly and things fall into place. It was like the solution to one of Kolya's puzzles, how the red and blue trains could pass each other on a single track without colliding.

Stevens was back on "Louisa" again. He took my notebook from me and wrote down: Chloroform.

Chloroform was what linked "Louisa" to his current investigation into the School of Jurisprudence. 'Chloroform leaves traces – blisters around the boy's mouth.'

That was their first mistake.

'All you need is a dribble. You hold it over the nose of the victim. If the victim panics and gulps the stuff down inadvertently, it could be fatal. That is where the doctor comes in. But what if there's a muddle and they get the wrong doctor, two men with the same name. When the doctor arrives he twigs to what's going on, but there are heavies in the room so he goes ahead, does the business with the chloroform, then panics and scoots out to flag down the nearest constable.'

Stevens had been working another story when he was accosted, 'by a fellow lugging a bloody great violoncello into the bar of the Foreign Press Club.'

It was what those in the trade called "an approach".

'He had a story for me; one no-one else would touch. I said, "Not here old man – the competition... Let's go somewhere private." He had brought with him a sworn statement from a doctor. I saw it with my own eyes. He was an intermediary representing certain interested parties. Powerful people. He intimated that he could put other documents my way – witness statements, depositions. What we were talking here was corruption at the highest level, depravity, a vice ring, the whole caboodle.'

What was shocking about it was that not a single one of those cases had come to trial. Stevens' services were needed to expose this scandal by syndicating the story abroad, beyond the reaches of the Russian censors.

32

'The Konradi connection is where you come in.' There was a contact, a source Stevens was keen to interview. This senator, another former classmate of Kolya's father, had spurned all Stevens' overtures and inducements – put bluntly, he wanted nothing to do with him. But Stevens wasn't to be put off so easily. Telling his story would be *therapeutic* he insisted, making a smash and grab for the latest medical jargon, before adding a touch of schmaltz for maximum effect, 'He needs to open his heart, shed a few manly tears.' You could almost hear "Hearts and flowers" in the background, hammed up on the violin.

'Why me?' I asked. Because deaf people make such good listeners. We only gave the *impression* of being an ace short of a deck!

I said I would think about it – an outright lie. Why risk putting Kolya under the spotlight when a walk-on part in Stevens' potboiler was in the offing? As things stood, the scandal Hoffmann was worried about was not going to materialise, so Kolya's reputation was secure.

Then why *did* I visit the senator? Was it because I couldn't get the image of that post-mortem kiss out of my mind? There was something missing, something linking Kolya and Pyotr Ilych, I hadn't yet got to the root of. If the senator had known both of them personally, this was something he just might be able to help me with. By way of setting myself a deadline, I wrote to Gerda with the news that I was nearly done and would be returning shortly.

33

Just as well I thought to ask Frau Ritter first, otherwise I would have been turned away at the border for having no papers. We had the map of "St Petersburg and Environs" spread on the card table in front of us while she explained that Finland was a separate territory and that, at the Belo-Ostrov crossing, I would be leaving one jurisdiction for another. She went to some trouble on my behalf the old girl, ferreting out the railway timetable, even checking the platform at the Finland Station.

'Just what you need, a trip to the countryside,' she said urging me on. 'I was only saying to Herr Ritter, "He's been looking a little cheesy lately, Theo has." '

"The Karelian Riviera" they called it in the brochures. "Dunes and white sand as far as the eye can see." If I was interested, she knew of a hotel in Terijoki, not German run, though friends of hers spoke well of it — the Bellevue. I didn't tell her about my post-Zoya aversion to the seaside.

Travelling in the early afternoon, I had a compartment to myself. To keep me occupied I had bought a *Petersburger Zeitung* from the kiosk near Gruber's in "Kraut heaven". I settled down with the free supplement and perused the classifieds for German-owned dachas.

"Pargolovo, June through July, suits solitary person, 200 rubles, furnished, comes with all services, 1 verst from river.

For sale: spades, hammocks, cutlery, storage cupboards.

Pavlovsk, summer concert programme at the Vauxhall Gardens and Ballroom..."

The headline article "To the Countryside, to Dachaland" was copy-writer's stuff, half sketch, half advertisement, not a patch on Walser's column in *The Illustrated Weekly*:

"Listless? Frustrated? Bored? Deafened by the echoing din of shovels and pick axes, of pile drivers and steam rollers? Choking on brick dust?"

I skim read the next few paragraphs: "Empty streets... shut-up houses... padlocked gates..." This would hardly do when writing to Gerda but I could, at a pinch make something of "sweet-smelling pine forests, ankle deep in mushrooms and fir cones... dunes, sea glimpses..."

Stepping down from the train I made a final adjustment to the knot in my tie. There was a gig waiting for me that whisked me to the dacha in less than five minutes.

I had got no further than the garden gate, when I found my way blocked by a bald, elderly man wearing braces and a collarless shirt, the sleeves rolled up to the elbows. He looked me up and down, then said, 'Well, I hope you don't mind getting your hands dirty.'

It was only when he was ushering me in the direction of a lean-to at the back of the house and yanking open the door that I remembered attaching a 'Theo Brand Cycles: new and repaired' card to Hoffmann's letter of introduction. (I saw it later propped against a silver salver on the sideboard.)

Did I look like a mechanic? Before setting out for the senator's I had jumped the queue for the boarding house hipbath, got a haircut, trimmed my beard with a special comb I bought in the Petrovsky Gallery and cut my nails. I had sent my shirts to the laundry and my best linen jacket to the dry cleaners. What greater pains could a man take with his appearance? (Admittedly I had let myself go a bit since Zoya buggered off out of my life, but he wouldn't have guessed that day.)

Brushing away the cobwebs the senator lit an oil lamp. In a corner, propped against the wall, was a Royal Enfield Premier with a few years on it. He took my jacket and gave me a long carpenter's apron he helped me tie at the back. The only thing wrong with the bike was the chain needed tightening and, as the

Premier is a 'fixie' with no derailleur complications, the job was done in a matter of minutes. Instead of standing idly by as I was expecting, the senator had been keen to lend a hand so I got him to hold the handlebars steady while I took out a link. Leading me back towards the house he patted me several times on the shoulder in a friendly gesture that was not quite natural, as if he had been shown how by a nanny or governess. I stopped at the pump to wash my hands with carbolic and took a gander at the house.

Frau Ritter had put it into my head to expect something rather grand, a villa or country estate but apart from an extra storey the senator's dacha was bog standard. It made me think of the slogan in the *Petersburger Zeitung*: "Build your own for a fraction of the price – subscribe to our catalogue now."

34

If I had not met the senator already, I would have known just from his tread that he had a light frame and walked with an even gait. He was drying his hands as he came back in while an old manservant stood by with a clean shirt.

'Aggravated assault wasn't it, a robbery that went wrong?'

I wasn't sure how to address him, Your High Excellency, or just plain Excellency. When I looked him up in in the library I discovered he had a title – count or baron, a proper one, not like "*Il Barone*". The name, von Waal was German-sounding. Frisian? Latvian? I wondered whether to mention my own Russian relatives but decided against it. If the senator could trace his family back to the Vikings, we were hardly on an equal footing.

'Yes, sir, aggravated assault.' It would do. Frankly I had grown tired of conspiracy theories and was relieved when the senator moved the conversation on to the family.

'I know they have been well provided for; all the same, if there is anything... How old is the boy?'

Six? Seven? I had to guess.

'Very hard on a boy, being left without a father. And the wife – am I right in thinking she's German? Then perhaps it will be for the best if they settle there permanently. In any case, if you do call on her...'

I said that of course I would pass on his condolences. I felt there was something lacking in me, that I was not coming across as enough of a pal to Kolya. So I told the senator about our chance meeting on the Gendarmenmarkt. It was a clumsy, humdrum account until by a happy chance a small detail came to me about Gunthermann's toy stall and watching Kolya explaining the winding mechanism of a model engine to his son.

Was it *Gemütlichkeit,* that put me at my ease, the cosiness of the surroundings? The geraniums on the table were my mother's favourite. Or was it the senator pouring the tea himself after Geronty had returned from the kitchen, holding the samovar aloft with both hands like a steaming silver trophy? I had let go of my hat without giving it a second thought. Even when the senator insisted I put my notebook away for the duration of the interview I refused to be cowed.

I had not eaten since breakfast to avoid getting grease spots on my tie and was beginning to feel hungry. I remember the aroma of grilled fish, wafting though the open back door from a neighbouring house and the pangs increasing as we moved onto the veranda. It was not the spread I had been looking forward to. Set before us instead was an assortment of nuts and berries, red apples with wrinkly skins and black bore holes, rye bread and porridge. To drink I was offered kvass, fermented mare's milk, or homemade cranberry juice. Health food – my host was a faddist! I had been invited to stay the night, but now found myself trying to recall the time of the last train back to St Petersburg. I would have to get a move on.

I started with the senator's assessment of Kolya's state of mind at the time of Pyotr Ilych's death. Varlamov had him behaving like a character in a melodrama, kissing the corpse and the rest of it. Did they really have to *drag* him away, or was this actor's licence?

The senator had not witnessed the scene in the apartment but he confirmed that Kolya was distraught.

'He knew from Pyotr Ilych himself that something was wrong but had put off coming until it was too late.'

I had to get this straight.

'Are you saying Pyotr Ilych wrote to him from his sick bed?'

'Konradi showed me the letter. I only saw it the once. Dashed off, judging from the handwriting and befuddled - like someone who had been drinking.'

The senator ate sparingly and with a disdainful expression on his face, like a man with a stomach ulcer or suffering from heartburn.

Every mouthful he washed down with kvass, as if under doctor's orders.

'Might it have been the fever, Sir?'

'I wondered about that too – only you see Pyotr Ilych was not ill when he wrote it. It was dated the Tuesday before the doctor was summoned.'

The senator pushed his bowl to one side and began rubbing a lotion onto the backs of his wrists to soothe the scaly eruptions on his skin. Eczema. Now I realised why he had left his shirt cuffs undone.

'Then if he wasn't ill, Sir, why the urgency? Another thing...how could Kolya possibly have known?'

'It was the reference to Antinous: "The friends of Antinous have taken against me."'

Antinous! My mind travelled back to my conversations with Hoffmann and Persiani, to the Villa Adriana in Tivoli, to the obelisk on the Pincian Hill with its obscure hieroglyphs and to the man-god himself, the handsome warrior who conquered the Emperor's heart before drowning mysteriously in the Nile and becoming the object of a mystery cult.

The senator quoted Hölderlin: "Warum huldigest du, heiliger

Sokrates diesem Jünglinge stets?"

It was a line from my school copybook. Why holy Socrates, do you revere only young men?

'Socrates answers: "He who thinks the deepest, loves what's most alive."

The "friends of Antinous" had started out as a school society. Antinous was chosen as patron because he represented the Greek ideal of beauty.

Members of the society read poems, gave talks, discussed books. A plaster cast of the Belvedere Antinous presided over meetings. All pretty innocuous, until Chersky started gaining the upper hand, insisting that the society be re-formed as an Order with Chersky himself as its high priest or "pontifex."

'He was to decide who were the neophytes and who were to be inducted into the higher mysteries.'

I thought of what Stevens had said about "calling to order"? They were in the Caffè Greco to meet Pontifex.

35

There is a moment around dusk when, as the light fades, even common-place objects – a watering-can or a garden rake – seem to take on a sinister aspect.

'These Greek notions of theirs...'

Greek notions? Did he mean to say *Greek Notions of Love*? I thought of the book Persiani had smuggled out of Modest Ilych's apartment on the Pincio and locked away in the embassy safe.

'It's nonsense to suggest we can turn ourselves into Ancient Greeks by process of osmosis, through mimicking their rituals, singing hymns of praise to the gods...'

Strange the senator talking about osmosis – the term was often banded about in Theosophical circles. What he was getting at, I think, was that it's impossible to see the world as Odysseus would have seen it.

The Order of Antinous reminded me of when Reuss joined the Order of the Eastern Temple.

I was beginning to see now how someone like Chersky might be capable of corrupting a society run by a bunch of tenth graders. In Reuss's case it started with mantras and joss sticks, then a guru comes along and the next thing you know it's smoking dope, toying with devil worship, and … practising Tantric sex I was about to add when I checked myself. This was my future brother-in-law I was talking about.

I shuddered, quite involuntarily. The senator, thinking I was cold, handed me a rug.

As the shadows lengthened on the overhanging eaves, the woodcarvings of birds and diamonds, the corner tower with a steeple like a sharpened pencil, the dacha was metamorphosing into the witch's cottage in Hansel and Gretel.

The senator was shaking the sediment at the bottom of his glass. 'They said the trips to Italy would broaden his horizons, provide him with a more rounded education than he had been getting at the School for the Deaf. Konradi's father took a lot of convincing but in the end they won him round. No doubt it was well intentioned.'

'You don't seem convinced Sir?'

'Let's just say that… a young boy away from home for months at a time. It was an unconventional household.'

Did Kolya think of Chateau Perache as home? I wondered about that.

'There was a governess, but it seems her services were dispensed with.'

I noticed there was no mention of Alina in all of this.

'An all male household.' The senator said it as a statement of fact. 'Pyotr Ilych had a servant, Voronov, who travelled with them.'

'Sofronov, you mean. Alyosha Sofronov.'

'As I said...I heard they gave him far too free a rein. He was insolent and over-familiar, not to mention spoilt rotten. Both the brothers were at fault in that regard. Pyotr Ilych was of a kindly disposition and could be taken advantage of, while his brother was weak. Servants of that age need a firm hand in my opinion.'

I had been wondering about Alyosha's status ever since visiting Klin. In the photograph on the mantelpiece, Alyosha might have been taken for a relative rather than a domestic, for one of the family.

'He was allowed to carouse with their friends, whether they were present or not. Kolya told me of one occasion when they put Sofronov in a tutu and sent him pirouetting about the room while they clapped and jeered.'

I was beginning to understand why Alyosha might have his own reasons for avoiding the attentions of prying journalists.

I helped myself to the last of the marinated mushrooms while waiting for the senator to pick up the thread of what he was trying to say.

'Pyotr Ilych, wanted nothing to do with Prince Chersky and his cronies. But when the Tchaikovsky's were in Rome for the carnival, his brother persuaded him that they would save money if they moved out of their hotel and rented a villa together. There was a day when Kolya was feeling under the weather, the others went sightseeing without him but Masalatinov returned early on some pretext and called on Kolya in his bedroom.'

The lotion on the senator's wrists must have been losing its effect because he was scratching at his eczema again.

'It was years before he could bring himself to talk about it and the strain took its toll, God knows.'

I was trying to imagine Kolya living with the fear that at any moment Masalatinov might reappear, corner him in some doorway or stairwell with no one to protect him.

'Children have a sense you know of when something isn't right, even when they can't put it into words.'

And when Kolya did finally speak out, it was just as he feared: there was an almighty row with Modest Ilych. Now, at last I was hearing Kolya's side of the story – Sofronov, as I had always suspected, had been lying. The cause of the rift was not Kolya's inheritance at all, but Modest Ilych's failings as a guardian.

Which left Pyotr Ilych. Here too the senator was surprisingly forthcoming. 'He didn't want to believe it and anyway it came at a bad moment – Tchaikovsky was distracted by the arrangements for his tour of America.'

Then my friend had no one else to turn to. No wonder he left Russia without a forwarding address.

'When he did come to realise that he too had let Kolya down, Pyotr Ilych was devastated. It was like losing a son.'

I wanted to tackle the senator head-on over something that had been bothering me all along.

I took a long draught of cranberry juice while deciding how best to broach it without causing offence.

'This is a network of paedophiles we're talking about Sir. I don't understand how they can be allowed to carry out their activities with impunity.'

The senator lit a cheroot while he thought the matter over. Then he emptied a bowl of nuts onto the tablecloth and held one up – this represented the Tsar. Placing it at the centre of the table, he pushed the rest to one side. These were the Duma and the Tsar's ministers. He then took half a dozen of the nuts and arranged them around "the Tsar" – Chersky and his associates in the court camarilla.

Camarilla I knew from the newspapers at home – the Eulenburg affair – a favourite of the Kaiser's had been accused of unduly influencing government policy. Chersky was using his position at court to protect his cronies.

But according to his letter, these same "friends of Antinous" had turned against Pyotr Ilych.

Was it because he had had the courage to defy the honour code of the School of Jurisprudence and confront Masalatinov? If it were ever to become public, the aftershocks could prove fatal to the reputation of the School.

Siskins. The students were called siskins, the senator said, because of the colour of their uniforms. I had seen a caged siskin in the dacha when I arrived. They were trapped – these former alumni – like birds in a cage. Chersky fed them through the bars; he might even open the door if the fancy took him and allow one to perch for a short while on his finger.

I was running my own finger back and forth along a crease in the tablecloth, when another image flashed through my mind – of Stevens riffling through his record cards. Surely Chersky too had been squirreling information, compromising material, intimate details.

Then the question was what hold Chersky might have had over Pyotr Ilych. His homosexuality? From what I understood, even in Russia the laws were rarely enforced, though being a commoner might have made him more vulnerable. Or could it have been his crazy marriage of convenience? The way Madame Blancmange had reported it, Tchaikovsky had got cold feet and panicked while still on his honeymoon. If the wife had refused to be bought off, then only someone with clout, a Chersky say, could have had her locked up in an asylum.   Or (and this would better explain Tchaikovsky's state of mind at the time of the letter) released – to be wheeled out like a surprise witness whose appearance sets off gasps and titters in the public gallery.

36

Geronty cleared away the tea things but the senator showed no sign of moving inside. Taking a cue from my host, I pulled the rug over my knees. Darkness seemed to be creeping up on us as if trying to take us by surprise; the trees too, advancing like the army in Shakespeare's play. Suspecting a confidence might be in the offing, I nudged the oil lamp closer by degrees so I could follow any disclosure more easily.

With a groan, the senator buried his head in his hands. 'I only wanted what was best...'

He faltered before trying again.

'I had such hopes for Sasha when I put his name down for the School. Think of what he might have achieved. Isn't that what every father wants for his son? And he seemed happy to be there...

'Then his mother noticed a change in him... he became sullen and withdrawn... No matter how gently she spoke to him, he would fly into the most terrible rages, screaming at her, even pummelling her with his fists.

'I decided to have it out with him, man to man. I wondered if he had done something against the rules, something of which he was ashamed. God forgive me, how could I have allowed myself to interrogate my own son as if I were a prosecutor cross-questioning a criminal? And then, not believing him, thinking it wasn't possible, I became angry, lost my temper, lashed out.'

He was tugging at his wedding ring, pulling and twisting as if he wanted to wrest it off his finger altogether.

'I shoved Chersky hard against the wall and watched him slither to the floor. "No child," I said, "should be left in the company of such vermin." '

The senator's son was being treated at a clinic in Vienna where he had spent much of the last ten years staring sightlessly into space, listless, apathetic and afraid of the future.

'Such monstrous behaviour... I would castrate them, not banish them at the Tsar's pleasure – Is this how you get rid of an infestation, wish it away?   I'll show you what "banishment" amounts to.'

He brought out a box file stuffed with papers. There were tinted postcards of Capri, Amalfi and the Bay of Naples, photographs of a crenelated villa on a cliff top with a staircase leading down to the beach where men in bathing costumes were drying off in the sun. The same men, posing with musicians outside a café. Among bills and receipts, more photographs – of street children with dates and places, and the letterhead of a detective agency in Naples.

This, the senator said, was "evidence".

'How can a child *lead someone on*? "I don't know what got into me, he made me do it." What kind of a defence is that, blaming the victim?'

I was completely at a loss and must have shown it, because he cried out, 'I want my son back, body and soul!'

It wasn't that I didn't feel for him, but what could I, what could anyone say? At least Kolya had kept his sanity.

BERLIN

1

Strange the way things work out, how discovering Kolya's secret has led to an outcome so – well, fitting. I have come to see a pattern in all these events, a design, as when an author planning a novel will get the ending right, then other things fall into place.

It was Kolya's box which gave rise to this story of mine. The seeds of its development, of how it would unfold were there in front of me – take the postcard with the obelisk, the one from 'P' who was "missing Kolya terribly" in 1887; in the light of what I have since discovered, 'P' must be Pyotr (Ilych). But, what if some of the clues were missing, if Kolya in his delirium had assumed mistakenly that the disturbing last letter from Pyotr Ilych was also in there?

Set against this is the impulsive way I created a new denouement that caught even me by surprise – by altering my travel plans, a decision made, I have to say, not from the best of motives. Where did the inspiration come from, me or Kolya? Choosing to do something so rash and last minute on Znamenskaya Ploschad, the 'Square on the Sign' was surely more than coincidence. No? Ah well.

It had become a habit, going to the station square every day to make my 'to do' lists. I still have the Russian pocket diary with the propelling pencil, the pages blank until *"31 July, Friday, sun rises at 9.06am and sets at 9.00pm"* Here I have written:

stamps, one sheet at 10 kopecks; one commemoration set with all the tsars, 5 roubles ✔

keys to Frau Ritter, with forwarding address ✔

haircut

break up 25 rouble note into small denoms. for tips and sundries ✔

toothpaste, hand lotion

Just seeing these lists again gives me the same giddy feeling I had as a child when Pop would announce, *'If* the weather holds, what do you say to a little outing to Rahnsdorf tomorrow?' (To me Rahnsdorf meant: rushing the deckhand to grab the front seats on the steamer, fighting for the binoculars with Gerda as we raced to the top of the viewing platform on Spindler's Tower, a splash-about in the Müggelsee and then a picnic with crusty bread, *bouletten* and Berliner *senf*!) It was the proviso about the weather that held me in thrall, through the night and well into the following morning when I would be on the doorstep at five minute intervals scrutinising the sky, as if an act of will would scour away the first advancing cloud.

There is nothing in the diary about trawling the gift shops on Nevsky Prospekt in a state of panic after realising that the souvenirs I had accumulated along the way would no longer do: three pairs of camiknickers courtesy of Lindstrom that I had originally earmarked for Reuss to give to a girlfriend; one photograph in a silver frame, signed (so the shopkeeper assured me) by Pavlova herself; one jar of marmalade from "Abrikosov's, confectioner to the court of Russia"; one wooden Dalmatian on wheels – company for Stammer Max(?); a ceramic plate, commemorating the tercentenary of the Romanov dynasty; a musical box with drawers that I had earmarked for myself (and paid for with my own money).

Yes I was anxious to get home. The trouble was I had too much time on my hands like Odysseus becalmed on the homeward leg, only *my* doldrums were of my own making. Why had I set aside *eight days* for excursions to Pavlovsk, Tsarskoye Selo and other Baedeker "must-sees"? If I'd been honest with myself, I should have known I would get no further than Gruber's and the Billiard Hall, where I was hell bent on recovering my losses by beating Ivanov at least once at 'Russian Rules'. (I never did.)

Another problem with having time on your hands – it leaves you vulnerable to unhealthy bouts of brooding. Alyosha Sofronov had wheedled his way into my subconscious like a string of gristle stuck in the teeth that no amount of contortions with the tongue can dislodge. What *was* it with him, pulling those faces in the Winter Garden restaurant when I was explaining about auras, as if taking a scientific interest in the occult was more ridiculous than wearing trinkets to ward off evil spirits? And those pretensions of his were laughable: as if Tchaikovsky would take his advice on the ending of an opera! But what I most objected to, what caused me most offence was him supposing that we were the same species, free-riding barnacles clinging to the hull of a cargo ship loaded with bullion. (I'm borrowing the image from Pop who liked to point out that these "parasites of the deep" literally have no hearts.)

But working myself into a lather wasn't going to get me anywhere.

What if I let my attack dog off the leash? Stevens would slaver at the prospect of tearing into Sofronov's pretensions. Or I could doorstep him myself...

If I were to take the midnight train to Moscow, stop off at Klin, spend the night in a hotel, then pick up the Petersburg-Berlin service in Warsaw I would still arrive home before my trunk.

2

The front door was open so I went in. Please God I thought, let me catch Sofronov out performing some menial task – polishing the furniture or ironing Modest Ilych's shirts. I felt a queazy glee, my stomach was heaving so violently I thought I might sick up my breakfast. I let my eyes adjust to the light then tried each door in turn. Everything was as I had remembered: the plant in the hallway, the stair carpet with the loose runner, the baby grand Kot had tinkled on for my benefit, the mantelpiece with the clock set at two minutes past three, Tchaikovsky's bedroom slippers. Everything, that is except the photograph, which was back where I had found it and not where Kot had told me it belonged. Were they playing games these custodians of Pyotr Ilych's memory – moving the objects in the house about like squabbling children?

Still no sign of Sofronov. I crossed to the alcove window from where Kot and I had watched him fumble with his door key. Looking down now I saw visitors gathering for a tour of the house. One of them, a young woman grown tired of waiting perhaps, broke away to pull a margarita from the side of the path, smuggling it into her basket when she thought no one was looking.

Spotting Kot, I went downstairs. He didn't exactly look pleased to see me but pointed to a room at the end of a short, unlit corridor, one I had not come across on my earlier visit.

3

At first I wondered if it was all a tasteless prank – dressing an effigy as if it were a living human being, going as far as to plant a tasselled cap on the shrunken head at a jaunty angle, then curling the bony fingers around the armrests of a wheelchair. Was Sofronov about to leap out from behind the curtain like the compere in the Pink Halls Cabaret?

No, I was alone with Modest Ilych.

I was staring. I knew it was wrong but I couldn't help it. His skin had turned sallow, like ancient parchment and someone, a practical joker (?), had applied carmine to the lips and a touch of rouge to the cheekbones so he looked like Kasper the puppet. An open book was lying on his lap, but his gaze was far away.

He noticed me and started. I became alarmed, thinking he might have mistaken me for a visitor who had strayed into a part of the house that was out of bounds. If I didn't explain myself, he would ring the bell and have me ejected.

I said who I was, but it meant nothing to him. It was only when I hit on "Chateau Perache" that we established a connection. He even started to sign, though what he said was largely unintelligible. At least we were communicating.

I took him to be asking about whether anyone had been charged with Kolya's murder and told him as much as I knew. He seemed more interested in what would happen with Grankino, whether Kolya had an heir. Clearly they had been unable to patch up their differences. His brother had craved a reconciliation; that was implied in the letter. Modest Ilych had his chance in Rome but nothing had come of it. Now it was too late.

I had been watching Kolya's former guardian closely, trying to decipher what he might be thinking. What was written on those pinched features of his? – bitterness, resentment, regret; certainly not remorse. Through the quilted dressing gown, tied loosely so that beneath the open waistcoat and the striped shirt no one had bothered to iron, you could make out the beating of a heart and lungs that worked in fits and starts like punctured bellows. But there was no fight left in him, no raging against the abyss that must now be opening up. It was difficult not to feel sorry for him.

There seemed little point in taxing the old man's patience further. I was on the point of leaving, when he signalled for me to help him get over to his desk. It meant manoeuvring the wheelchair. Even for a novice I made a poor fist of it and there was at least one collision before we reached our goal.

He took a key from the pocket of his dressing gown, unlocked one of the drawers and drew out a single sheet of manuscript paper. It shook violently in his hand as he turned to face me. He was holding on to my arm – not for support but for emphasis; I was to pay attention. He was anxious to take the credit for giving Pyotr Ilych's last symphony the title of *Pathetique*. His pride would have been understandable if he had not been so insistent. It was the way he emphasised each syllable: *Pa-the-tique* that made me wonder if it had once been a matter of dispute.

I knew all about the history of the sixth symphony from talking to Varlamov. The audience at the premiere had found the ending baffling. It left a sombre and gloomy impression. Tchaikovsky's public had been expecting a rousing finale, not an *Adagio* that began with what seemed to be snatched sobs. His death, coming only a week later, was reassuring in a way, it gave the movement a sinister premonitory significance, like Mozart's Requiem. There were clues in the score, the critics said, if you looked closely enough.

Modest Ilych scorned these claims – what did these people know about his brother's intentions? He was clear in his mind. Pyotr Ilych's symphony was a declaration of love.

He handed the page of manuscript to me, but held on to one corner. I recognised Tchaikovsky's handwriting from the manuscripts Kot had showed me on my first visit. He had written:

"Symphony Pathetique by Pyotr Tchaikovsky. Op.??? To Nikolai Pavlovich Konradi."

That was something to take in, but Modest Ilych had not finished. He seemed to be grimacing – was he in pain? Surely he can't have been smiling?

He wanted to tell me about Sofronov. Modest Ilych had been hiding the manuscript from him, that was why he kept the key in his pocket. I told him he needed to slow down if I was to understand. Something about a substitution. Sofronov had gone to the Post Office with the finished symphony after inserting another dedication page in the name of a relative. It was seeing Kolya's name that had driven him to this reckless action. After publication, Modest Ilych got the truth out of Sofronov and insisted he hand over the original page. Now Modest Ilych saw an opportunity to thwart the upstart servant by giving the dedication to its rightful owner, Kolya's son. It was for me to see that it was smuggled out of the house so Sofronov could not destroy it on Modest Ilych's death.

He was wheezing and short of breath. I eased the manuscript free before he could change his mind. He was waving me away as I closed the door on Klin for good.

4

It was hardly the Kroll Theatre – number seven on the list of venues Reuss had inspected at my request. I wondered if he was getting as tired of the whole business as I was. At least there was a definite spring in his step as he set off down the aisle, clapping vigorously as if trying to provoke some movement in the sluggish air or re-capture a stray bird on the wing. Acoustics not being my forte (as Reuss was not slow to point out), I hung back tactfully in the shadows, resting my weight on the back of a chair while I waited for the verdict.

Dry, did he say?

Dry. Insufficient resonance. The strings must be able to sing, to *breathe*.

I should have left it all to him – he was the musician after all.

I had originally intended to take on all the planning myself and give Gerda, Reuss and the rest of them cause to marvel at my efforts. In my own mind I was a revamped product: "new, improved". But I soon had to admit I had overestimated my organisational skills. Herr and Frau Reuss-to-be suggested I submit a plan for discussion. I did. Gerda's verdict: there were "shortcomings" (Reuss put it more strongly). First off – under the heading 'musicians': why, Reuss wanted to know, was there nothing about scores, performance fees, music desks, rehearsal schedules etc etc.? Gerda wondered about invitations, refreshments, flowers...

On the point of being squeezed out altogether, I insisted on choosing the venue. At this point we agreed to form a steering committee, Gerda preferring to describe it as a "pow wow", Reuss the grand-sounding "triumvirate".

My plan had also omitted any mention of a date. Gerda consulted the calendar and we opted for Sunday 28 June. Gerda's wedding had to take priority even if it meant missing the anniversary of Kolya's death by a mile.

The months rolled by and it still wasn't the Kroll Theatre but the Garrison Church Hall, Hasenheide and we were fortunate to get that at such short notice – pushing his luck as usual, Reuss had tried for the church itself, arguing that the music to be performed, while not, strictly speaking sacred (or religious he might have added) was "spiritual in nature" but the chaplain was not to be fooled.

In a manner of speaking, the concert was Kolya's idea. He conveyed it to me on the train as I was staring out of the window while being lulled to sleep by the rocking motion of the carriage. I was vaguely aware that it was beginning to get light and I remember we were somewhere near Posen. The book I was holding must have slipped from my fingers because it was the dull thud that woke me up. Had I read it or imagined it? Something about pacifying the soul of a man who died a violent death and whose protesting spirit refuses to cross over into the next world. What if I were to arrange a performance of the symphony? Would that set his soul to rest? It would be a parting gift, to him and to me, my own 6th Symphony.

5

Some homecoming! No-one to meet me at the station as I struggled with my bags. Not even a note of greeting on the front door. No sign of Strammer Max either. I was a bit put out I have to admit but all Gerda had to say on the matter was, 'Well, sorry your highness but some of us have been out at work all day, not gallivanting around Europe.'

Then, before she'd even taken off her coat: 'I've got a surprise for you.' And we were on the street again. Reuss was waiting for us outside a house on Bergmannstrasse, a few doors down from the market hall. Disgruntled but keen for them to get on with it, I followed obediently into the second courtyard, third left where Reuss dug out a set of keys. A poorly-lit hallway led to a stone staircase. I had counted to ten flights when I looked up to see Gerda beaming at me from a turn in the stairwell. They took me on a tour of inspection. 'And this is your room. Well, what do you think? It's a bit dear, but we'll manage I expect if we club together...'

She was glad to see me, of course she was but her wedding was the top priority now: the church was booked, I should see the flowers, Heini had been an angel about the dress. ("Well it's not every day you hear wedding bells and it's for you, is it?" chimed in a nurse from the Charité who had popped in to see the wayward brother for herself.)

The first Saturday, I had gone round to Gerda's old place on Yorckstrasse to collect my post. She had had it redirected there while I was away. Bills, flyers, orders, queries – they could all wait as far as I was concerned, until after breakfast at least. I had brought the *Morgenpost* with me. There was an article I hadn't finished reading about the role of the bicycle by a military strategist. In a future war, so the strategist predicted the bicycle would be a vital part of the war effort, ferrying the injured to hospitals and first aid stations, getting men from A to B, carrying supplies and equipment across rough terrain, taking messages...

I looked up to see Gerda standing over me, coffee pot in hand. It smelt good I must say.

'Will you be going in later?' she wanted to know. 'I don't want you and Strammer Max getting under my feet.'

I rubbed my chin as if giving the matter a great deal of thought. 'Maybe I'll sort through the correspondence – see if there's anything urgent. Josef can open up, or the new help – Whatshisname.'

But Josef hadn't been well. Besides the customers had been

asking about me. They wanted to know where I'd been all that time. And did she tell them?

'Of course not, it's too far fetched for words. I said you were abroad visiting a sick relative.'

'Anyone I know? Just in case they ask...'

I was grinning, she was not.

'You're out of the habit of working – *da liegt der Hund begraben!*'

That was the truth of the matter. It was good to hear Berlin slang again.

6

I have no definite plans – what would be the point? It was while I was circulating, doing the rounds of our VIPs – Persiani, Hoffmann (minus Claudia) and Kolya's widow and young son, Lukas – when news came of the assassination of the Archduke and his wife in Sarajevo. It caused a bit of a kerfuffle but as Balkan politics had been in the news for so long, no one expected it to lead to anything but another diplomatic crisis. Maybe if I had been in Trieste I would have paid more attention. As it was the performance went ahead as scheduled, beginning with Tchaikovsky's Italian Capriccio and concluding, after a short interval with the sixth symphony. The orchestra were 'scratch' musicians though good ones and Reuss himself conducted.

For the time being at least I will stay put in the house on Bergmannstrasse, but I am reserving the right to pull out of the arrangement if there is a change in my situation.

I have had one tempting offer. Hearing from my old teacher, Freycinet, was the last thing I expected. He wrote a friendly letter suggesting I join the staff of the school in Rome (after training it goes without saying). I am excited by the idea and might well take him up on it when hostilities end. In the meantime I am toying with the idea of taking on a deaf apprentice – in a small way this would be acknowledging Kolya's work for the deaf cause.

As for my ladies, I have given them up for the present, although I am still being recommended.

I also intend to write an account of my travels (some of the notes are in front of me now).

I am thinking of sending it to the principal of "Chateau Perache" for publication in the newsletter they issue from time to time. My hope is that it will encourage future pupils to rise to whatever challenges life presents, with fortitude and Berlinish *chutzpah*.

Gerda is mistaken about Kolya. Far from wasting a year of my life (she exaggerates as usual), I found a new way to live, living in and for the moment, being aware of living. That's what "seizing the day" really means. It's for me to decide how I live my life so long as I use my freedom responsibly, without encroaching on the freedom of others; that is where the harm is done.

And while it is true that our friendship was a relatively short one, confined more or less to our years at school, it is no less valuable to me for that. I owe it to Kolya for counting on me to protect his son from the revelations that might otherwise have hurt or harmed him. And I did not let him down.

It was while I was sitting in the concert hall that my thoughts had turned to Antinous and his – what was the word Persiani used? – Apotheosis: Antinous transformed, deified by the decree of a grieving, loves-struck emperor. Antinous immortalised in love. Now Kolya too, I thought, had been touched by immortality, his spirit flowed in the music like a droplet carried on a stream.

Sometimes I read to Kolya. This is in line with the latest thinking of the Theosophists who argue that between death and rebirth, comes a transitory state in which the dead may become confused and encounter obstacles to their spiritual progress. This is especially the case when, in life, they have spent too much of their time and attention on material things. It is not necessary to read to them aloud, only to concentrate, to focus intently on the content. It helps to picture the deceased person while you are reading, as if he was alive, sitting or standing in front of you.

I will read to him again tomorrow...

35794329R00211

Printed in Poland
by Amazon Fulfillment
Poland Sp. z o.o., Wrocław